"What has happened to the old ones, that they send us swimmers who are so unready?"

asked Boroni.

"Perhaps they have no choice," Rintu said. "Perhaps the sea is no longer kind to hatchlings and swimmers."

Boroni picked up a wand and whipped it at the encroaching bushes. Rintu could imagine his scowl. "Then..."

Boroni did not finish, and Rintu shared his unvoiced fear. Without waterlives, their kind would perish.

A clump of lupods marked a division of the trail and Boroni disappeared into the shadows. Rintu stared after him, troubled, until a rustle of undergrowth made him turn. In the glow of the lupods he stared down into a pair of frightened eyes.

The small creature froze. It was the swimmer he and Jass had left for dead on the beach. Rintu marveled: a miracle, for it to be here.

He looked more closely. Her newskin, unoiled, was puckered and blistered, and her mouth was blue. The cold would finish her during the night, Rintu thought, watching as she shivered spasmodically. A pity, for one who had survived such odds.

On an impulse he threw her his cloak. Then he ran off, before he could change his mind.

WATER SONG

WATER SONG

MARY CARAKER

POPULAR LIBRARY

An Imprint of Warner Books, Inc.

A Warner Communications Company

Popular Library books are published by
Warner Books, Inc.
666 Fifth Avenue
New York, N.Y. 10103

 A Warner Communications Company

Printed in the United States of America

First Printing: September, 1987

10 9 8 7 6 5 4 3 2 1

To Emmett,
and to the friends at Tierra Del Mar

Part I

OUT OF
THE CRADLE

1

Two suns, one brilliant and one a faint white glimmer, shone above a crescent of steeply sloping beach. Behind dunes covered with webgrass stretched forested mountains as boundless as the sea that battered the shoreline.

In the swells beyond the waves, dark specks moved slowly to the land. A watcher on one of the dunes caught sight of them and ran shouting into the forest.

"They are coming! The swimmers are coming!"

Rintu heard the shout as he lay half drowsing beneath his name tree, and he sat up abruptly. "It's much too soon for a landing," he muttered to himself. He gathered the handful of nuts he had found before he had succumbed to an hour of rare laziness, dropped them into his belt pouch and set off at a run for the shore.

Other landlings emerged from the forest. His friend Boroni waved a greeting, and Rintu joined him.

"They are early again. Too early," Boroni said. He frowned, and the scar tissue on his forehead formed lumpy ridges. Boroni's newskin had never formed properly. He had landed out of season himself, with no one to assist him, and he still bore the external marks of his ordeal.

Rintu's own gray skin was smooth and shiny over his hairless ovoid head. He was less muscular than Boroni, but his long legs easily kept pace. "It's the cold," Rintu said as he ran. He searched the sky for Smallsun, but though there were no clouds over the water he could discern only a dim glow. He could remember it eye-burning bright, some twenty cycles back when he had landed. Overhead, Bigsun shone fiery as usual, but beyond the shelter of the trees and the dunes the ocean wind whipped away its warmth.

Rintu shivered and drew his fur cloak about his shoulders. They stood on the open beach, watching the bobbing heads of the swimmers as they struggled to shore. Jutting black rocks defined the channel, and within it the current surged and swirled. Overhead, circling skyhunters waited for a mishap and a meal.

Rintu knew every curve and cove of the two-mile stretch of coast that was the lifeline of his tribe. The rocky barrier extended landward in a ridge that cut off his view to the north, but in his mind he could see clearly beyond it: the marshes that should have been verdant with life-sustaining seagreens; then more of the black rock, flat now and indented with sea-filled basins; the largest, their birthpool, opening to the ocean.

The eggs in the birthpool had become hatchlings and then swimmers, and now, after four season cycles in the water, they were ready to begin a new existence.

Rintu watched the wave-buffeted specks slowly grow larger. One struck the rocks, lay still, and a skyhunter swooped. Boroni shook his head and frowned again. "It will be worse than last time," he predicted. "It is much too soon for them to lose their waterskins."

Old Jass joined the two males. She pursed her mouth and made disapproving sucking noises. "They will be small," she grumbled, "and we will have to look after them again. The last ones couldn't even find their own food, remember? We had to show them how to do everything."

"We need no more weaklings," Boroni agreed. "If any of these appear unable to take care of themselves, it might be best to leave them on the beach."

"No, we should throw them back to the ocean to grow some more." Jass cackled at this, her idea of a joke.

Rintu looked at her with ill-concealed aversion. Jass was grossly fat, and her skin had begun to thicken in scaly patches. Soon she would be going back to the water herself, but she was making a bad change.

"No one had better touch my stores." She bared her teeth and tried to claw a hand that was already finlike.

Rintu turned away. He had mated with Jass not long ago, before her change had begun. Now he could not bear to think of it.

Boroni pressed Rintu's arm and pointed. The first of the swimmers were coming in on the crest of a foaming wave. It toppled them as it broke, pounding them into the seabottom. A few crawled to shore, but most were sucked out again as the wave withdrew.

The new landlings, four in all, lay gasping and flopping on the sand. They looked better than Rintu had expected. Their newskins were still raw and their limbs flabby, but they appeared to be almost fully grown. These were the largest and strongest, however; the first to survive the waves and the rocks and the skyhunters. Those still battling the surf would, he feared, be much less mature.

Rintu and Boroni and Jass joined the group around the first arrivals, smearing their newskins with oil and helping them to stand. Boroni supported a limp but well-formed figure. "This one will be picking his own dinner by nightfall," he said, chuckling, as he led the new tribe member away.

The second wave of swimmers to wash ashore proved as unpromising as Rintu had foreseen. They were pitifully small, and some had limbs bruised and broken by the rocks. One even had gill-slits not completely overgrown. They lay half in the water, choking but barely able to lift their heads. No one moved to help them.

"Hatchlings!" Jass spat out her disgust, and others echoed

it. Three of the uninjured ones managed to crawl to the tide-line, where they were succored, but those too weak to make it were left where they lay. Rintu thought of the skyhunters and shuddered, but he too turned his back. There was no place in the tribe for a landling who would be nothing but a burden.

He helped carry the last of the exhausted survivors to a windless pocket between the dunes. Two males and one female, they opened their eyes as they revived and gazed fearfully at the squatting figures who surrounded them. One by one they rolled from their stomachs to sit up.

They would be acceptable, Rintu thought, undersized though they were. Most likely they would have to be carried to the village, but they would be walking soon. He had stridden from the beach himself, as had most from his hatching, but that had been when the ocean was warm and he had lived longer in his waterskin.

Rintu and his companions exchanged nods. "They can stay in my house tonight," Marek said. He was the tribe's chief hunter, and his words carried authority. "One meal—if we all give something?"

The others agreed and rose to assist the new landlings to their untried legs. Rintu's arm was not needed, and he walked back to the beach for a final look.

"Pagh! Go back—we don't want a runt like you." Jass, standing alone, shrieked as she kicked at a wrinkled red figure still covered with patches of waterskin. The puniest landling Rintu had ever seen—upright, it would come barely to his waist—had managed to crawl halfway up the beach and fasten its hands around Jass's ankle. She picked up a stone.

Rintu wrested it from her. "No need for that. Leave the hatchling—it will die by itself."

The red figure had loosened its grip and lay still. At the water's edge knots of skyhunters feasted, and Jass looked from them to her intended victim. She shrugged. "You're right. But what an abomination it is." She took Rintu's arm as they started up to the dunes, dragging her feet and breathing with labored gasps.

Rintu suffered the touch. He would pity her, he thought, if she weren't so mean-spirited. In normal times one like her would already be spending hours in a warm tidal pool, perhaps even welcoming the final change. Rintu remembered his own time as a swimmer as a long idyll, and the old ones who had drifted with the hatchlings through the waving seagreens had seemed content, too. But now, with the water colder each season . . . no wonder Jass was resisting so fiercely.

In the forest, Jass went her own way and Rintu hurried to Marek's house. He would share his rintu nuts with the newcomers, fulfilling his promise, and at the same time get another look at them. The female had appeared rather attractive, for all her raw newness.

It was a long walk, for the houses of the village were widely scattered. Massive, gnarled trees towered above Rintu's head, spreading their protective branches over the occasional hut nestled at the base of a broad trunk. Rintu recalled his own first entry into the village, his wonder that it had been exactly as he had seen it in the watersongs of the old ones; leafy paths soft underfoot, a clear pond and a sunlit meadow and a separate dwelling for each member of the tribe. Everything so perfect and so right.

Marek's house was larger than most; he needed space for his horns and skins and dried meat. Instead of leaning on one tree wall, it stretched between two supporting trunks. The side walls were built up in the usual fashion of branches and clay and hides, with the roof of woven leaves on crosspoles.

Rintu stooped to enter and found it already crowded with three of the newcomers and Marek and Boroni.

The two older males, reclining on hides, shifted to make room. Even seated they were a sharp contrast in physical types: Marek slight, with a hunter's sinewy body; Boroni the stonecutter overwhelming by sheer bulk. They held themselves stiffly, as if interrupted in midquarrel.

The new landlings huddled together at the far end of the hut. Their bodies had been oiled and their skins were beginning to take on a more healthy gray hue, but they still looked to Rintu somehow unfinished. Their ridged necks supported heads that seemed disproportionately large, especially that of the female as her crest began to dry and stand out.

Rintu could not keep from staring. Even in the shadows the new female's crest scales gleamed with hints of red and gold that would be magnificent, he knew, in the sunlight. Her face, too, held a promise of beauty, with a soft mouth and large clear eyes. She sat spread-kneed, her sex a tightly folded bud.

"I've named her," Marek said. "Nithrin. The red pond flower. What to you think?"

Rintu struggled to appear unaffected. "A good name choice. But it will be some time before this flower opens for you, or for anyone else. They are all very young."

"I told Marek it was a mistake to bring them here," Boroni said. "We have never housed the new ones overnight before. If they cannot provide for themselves . . ."

"How many are there outside?" Rintu asked.

Boroni held up one four-fingered hand. "You saw them. The one I brought in has even started on a shelter. Not a bad one, either."

"That is the way it should be," Rintu agreed. "But there were so few strong ones this time. These three could never live unprotected through the night." He turned to Marek. "Are they walking yet?"

Marek shook his head. "But they will be by morning; I'm sure of it." He added Rintu's nuts to the small pile of fruit and seagreens in front of the newcomers and narrowed his eyes at Boroni. "One night only. Why should it disturb you?"

"It is not the custom." Boroni squared his shoulders and glared back at Marek. "Nor is choosing a name before the ceremony."

"It seems more important to me to assure that there will

be a ceremony," Marek said. "Remember last time, how many died?"

Boroni did not respond. His eyes strayed to the female and away quickly, suggesting that his concern for breach of custom was at least partly a subterfuge. Nithrin's first mating, Rintu thought, would result in more than one bloody head.

The newcomers began to eat. Rintu nodded to Marek. "A good sign. I say you have done well." He had no reason to stay longer, and followed Boroni out.

Bigsun had gone to rest, and Smallsun shone in the east with a ghostly light that did not warm. It should have been a long-day, Rintu reflected bitterly as he pulled his cloak tightly about him. They were into the season, but Smallsun was no longer strong enough to hold off the night, even for a few hours.

Boroni continued to grumble as he and Rintu followed a winding dark-shadowed trail. "I had no such comforts on my first night, nor did you or any of our hatching. Nothing saved us but our wits and what we knew from the teachers. What has happened to the old ones, that they send us swimmers who are so unready?"

"Perhaps they have no choice," Rintu said. "Perhaps the sea is no longer kind to hatchlings and swimmers."

Boroni picked a wand and whipped it at encroaching bushes. Rintu could imagine his scowl. "Then . . ."

Boroni did not finish, and Rintu shared his unvoiced fear. Without waterlives, their kind would perish.

A clump of lupods marked a division of the trail. "Until tomorrow," Rintu said as they separated.

Boroni did not return the sign. "No, this is one ceremony I will miss." His tone remained bitter. "Marek has started the naming already. He and others can finish it."

Boroni disappeared in the shadows. Rintu stared after him, troubled, until a rustle of undergrowth made him turn. In the glow of the lupods he stared down into a pair of frightened eyes.

The small creature froze. It was the swimmer he and Jass

had left to die on the beach. Rintu marveled: a miracle, for it to be here. And standing, walking. There must be surprising strength in that unformed body.

He looked more closely. The newskin, unoiled, was puckered and blistered and oozing blood in places. She was a female, with an unmistakable tight bud but no sign yet of a crest.

Her mouth was blue and she shivered spasmodically. The cold would finish her during the night, Rintu thought. A pity for one who had survived such odds.

On an impulse he threw her his cloak. An insane gesture, he knew. Probably useless, too—he could tell from the stinging skin on his bare shoulders and arms that there would be ice in the open places by morning.

He ran home before he could change his mind.

2

In his own hut, curled under a thin mossblanket, Rintu regretted the cloak. It had been a spotted chulafur, and he had been lucky to have come by it. He had little skill in hunting, and Marek would make him trade dearly for another. He would reclaim the cloak as soon as he could, he decided—whether or not the small one still lived. He had already done too much for her. The tribe would never accept such a one, and it was no kindness to prolong a life that could be nothing but misery. His stomach growled, and he regretted the nuts, too.

His thoughts moved to the next day's naming ceremony. Only seven new landlings. Fewer each time. He recalled his own naming, when he had been one of so many that the clearing had been packed. What would happen to the tribe when no more swimmers came to shore? What would happen to Jass and others as they turned into old ones if they could no longer return to the ocean? And what would happen to the hatchlings with no old ones to warn them of poisonous greens and rocks where killerfish hunted, to sing to them of life on shore?

Rintu fell at last into a fitful sleep. He was a swimmer again, sleek in his waterskin, gliding the currents. He heard the song of old Astar as she followed him: a sound-picture of golden beaches and sun-dappled forests and graceful creatures who walked on legs. The longing grew in him until he began to twist to rid himself of the waterskin which had suddenly become a constricting cage.

He awoke thrashing amid shreds of his blanket. The dream lingered in fragments, a life that was as distant to him now as the retreating Smallsun. It seemed that Astar had been trying to tell him something important, but try as he might he couldn't recapture the sense.

He gave up; it was useless to puzzle over dreams. Kicking the torn moss into a corner, he crawled out of his hut. It was small compared to Marek's—one could stand upright only in the tree end—but it was snug and well chinked. The treewall was wide, with low branches over a tightly woven roof.

Rintu adjusted his loin wrap and wished again for his cloak. Bigsun shone dimly through clouds and Smallsun was still resting. Frost spiked the open patches of tallgrass, and in the forest shade, leaves and vines hung swollen with icy moisture that dripped on him as he searched for his breakfast.

A half-hour's foraging yielded only a handful of berries. He ran into Pellen, whose hut stood in the same grove. She was their best climber and had had better luck, and he traded half the berries for a portion of sweet treegourd.

They ate as they walked together to the clearing. Rintu had meant to save his food for the naming feast, but he was too hungry to wait. Pellen was better prepared, carrying on her belt a marsh tuber wrapped in leaves. She had dressed carefully, too, adorning her long muscular arms with strands of shells that tinkled as she moved.

Though nearly everyone was assembled, there was room to spare in the meadow. Fifty-some landlings, in two rows, circled the seated newcomers. Rintu and Pellen took places, and Jass, as the oldest female, began the chant.

Lors the headman, in his white cape, crouched over the fire heating the carved stone. As the newcomers were led to him—even the three smallest walking well on their own—he branded each on the tender newskin of the shoulder. All bore the pain without a cry, and Rintu joined the press of well-wishers and namers.

Boroni, he saw, had changed his mind and come. The big stonecutter appeared to have lost his ill humor, and even joined in the naming. "Roko," he suggested for the largest male, the one he had befriended. "The name has always been lucky."

There was agreement, the last Roko having been a good forager and curer of hides.

Rintu studied the remaining unnamed ones. One female had a pointed face and a flat brown crest that suggested fur. "She looks like a tree cuma," he whispered to Pellen. "And we need another good climber."

Pellen nodded and shouted the name.

It stuck. Marek presented Nithrin as already named, and one by one all six of the newcomers acquired landling titles.

There should have been seven. Rintu knew what must have happened, but he put off asking.

Finally Marek confirmed his fears. "One died in the night. Or was killed. Lors found a half-eaten body by the spring."

It was worse than he had thought. "Not skyhunters, surely, in the forest. Could it be shureks?"

"Perhaps, though no one has seen them so near. It could also have been a natural death, and some other animal found the body. These swimmers were so young."

Rintu thought of the unnamed one who wore his cloak. It was hopeless for her, when even the new tribe members might not survive. "How will they manage, especially those three you sheltered?"

Marek kicked at a knotted clump of tallgrass. "Nithrin and the smaller male, Dak—the one with the limp—

I've . . ." He looked up with defiance. "They will remain with me another night. Until they build shelters and learn the ways. What is the harm?"

"None that I can see." Rintu could ill afford to judge.

Marek relaxed. The crowd was now centered about the fire, which smoked with roasting tubers. Boroni wrestled with Roko and took a mock fall, to laughter. Pellen started the name-dance and a few others, including Nithrin, followed. Dak and Cuma burned their fingers on tubers and learned the word "hot."

Perhaps he and Marek were worried unduly, Rintu thought; the newcomers seemed to be adapting well. And it could be a blessing that there were so few, with both the seagreen beds and the forest withholding their bounty. He wondered again about the little female. He was surprised that there had been no mention of another corpse. He looked around the edges of the clearing, half expecting to spot someone hidden there, watching.

He saw nothing, however. A rumble from the sky and a sudden downpour doused the fire and the festivities. Everyone ran for the trees.

"When will you be hunting again?" Rintu asked Marek as they gained the shelter of the forest.

Marek shrugged. "Maybe in a few days, for meat—I have enough skins now. Do you need one? I see you have lost your cloak."

"What would you trade for?" They started for Lors's house, keeping close under the trees. Dak and Nithrin followed—at a suitable distance, Rintu noted approvingly. Not intrusive, but close enough to watch and listen and learn.

The tribe regrouped in front of the headman's house, beneath a great triple-trunked gourd tree. The thunder continued, but the natural canopy of broad leaves protected them from the worst of the storm. "A bad omen for a nameday," Rintu heard whispered, but despite the portent the prevailing mood was one of determined gaiety. The roasted tubers had been rescued and were passed around, along with gourds and a single bowl of stewed meat and seagreens.

Not a mouthful apiece, Rintu thought. He had contributed nothing, so he did not eat, but those who did seemed to him scarcely better filled than he was. He did drink from the klava jar, and the warmth spread outward from his stomach.

"Hah! Not much of a feast, is it?" Jass squatted next to him, arranging her bulk awkwardly. She reached for the bowl and ate twice her share.

"There should at least have been more seagreens," agreed Marek. "Who went for them?"

"I did, and some others." One-eyed Krull put down the klava jar and spun around. "If you have complaints, go yourself and see the beds. Dying. And worse: a thief was there. A swimmer, or so it looked, taking greens for itself."

"A swimmer? So near shore?"

"In our beds? How could it cross the sandflats?" Shocked responses came from a dozen throats.

Krull's face darkened. "Don't you believe me? I tell you it was a swimmer, though it walked on legs. It had to be—it was barely this high." He held out his arm.

There were gasps. "It had a waterskin?"

"I couldn't tell; it was wrapped in a chulafur. Marek, you had better count your skins."

Marek looked at Rintu sharply. Rintu felt the heat in his face, but said nothing. Jass pressed his arm and shrieked, "It is the one! The land hatchling, the abomination! You should have let me kill it yesterday." She turned to Krull. "Where is it now?"

"We drove it away, across the sandflats. But it had already stolen most of the standing greens. We should guard the beds until we can be sure the robber is gone."

There was talk of this, but the rain continued and no one volunteered to go. The jar of klava went around again, and the seagreen beds became a distant problem, too far away to worry over. Everyone joined in more chants, Marek led a spear dance and Krull told a long rambling joke about a time when Smallsun vanished for the length of a landlife. It soon became clear he had forgotten the ending.

The few who listened responded with indulgent laughter,

for Krull was known for his maunderings. Rintu gave it little attention, concerned with his own crowd-pleaser—an inspired imitation of a longbill squawking and hopping on one leg. He rewarded himself with more klava; from then on nothing was clear to him until late in the day when Pellen came into her rutting. He was inflamed as soon as he smelled the musk, and fought wildly with Boroni and Marek and Lors and half a dozen others. Then the klava took over and he lay where he fell, unaware of who was the victor.

When he awoke in the morning, he was covered with his best chulafur. Everyone was gone except Boroni, who was sitting up with his hands to his head. "A shurek's piss, that klava!" he said, groaning.

Rintu silenced him, pointing to Lors's closed doorflap. He urged Boroni to his feet.

Rintu's own head throbbed, and he longed for seagreens. "Let's see if Krull was right about the marshes," he suggested once they were beyond Lors's tree space.

Bigsun was high in the sky by the time they reached the beach, but the seagreen beds were still ice-rimmed. Krull had spoken the truth: the marshes that had always been lush with the fleshy stalks were bare and brown, the new growth rotted before it could ripen.

Rintu pulled one of the healthier-looking sprouts, chewed it and spat.

Boroni did likewise, and cursed. They returned to the beach with muddy feet and no ease for their heads and stomachs. The wind whipped at them, and they sheltered in the dunes. "Lors should have known about the greens," Boroni said. "We should long ago have searched out a new patch."

"Maybe." Rintu looked toward the west where the far sun would normally be appearing. "But none of us expected Smallsun to hide this way. Did you hear Krull's story about the other long cold?"

Boroni shrugged. "Who listens to half of what that one says? He is too close to his change to think clearly—he and Lors both." He leaned close to Rintu, though there was no one to overhear. "We should be thinking now of a new headman, and not leave the choice to Lors. Someone in midspan —seasoned, but with a good number of cycles remaining."

"Someone like you?" Rintu couldn't help smiling.

Boroni ignored the teasing. "Either of us would serve the tribe well. Marek expects the honor, I know, but there are many who distrust him. This coddling of the newcomers—"

"Marek knows what he does." Rintu would hear no more. Of his two friends, he considered the thoughtful Marek a better candidate for headman than the proud and quick-tempered Boroni. As for himself, he wanted no part of such leadership. All he had ever sought from his landlife was comfort, with enough food and rutting females and no more adventure than an occasional mating fight. At the moment, the prospect of still having to search for his breakfast troubled him more than who would be the next headman.

Boroni stalked off in offended dignity, and Rintu followed. Muscales, he thought. Perhaps the vines in the grove by the pond would be bearing . . .

Boroni stopped, and Rintu caught up with him. Two figures were just emerging from the forest. In the open, they paused and looked around, and Rintu recognized them as Nithrin and Dak.

Nithrin pointed, and the two walked toward the seagreen beds.

Boroni called and motioned them back. "No use. There is nothing there.

"There is no food there," he explained again when they turned around and hesitated. They both wore body wraps of new hide, Dak awkwardly and Nithrin with surprising grace for one unused to clothing.

Dak twisted in his stiff skirt and rubbed his stomach. "Eat. Want eat."

Nithrin pulled him by the arm. "Come. Marek has eat. Marek give." She smiled, and her face had all the sweetness of her name flower.

Boroni stiffened. "She's a smart one." He growled the words. "She knows Marek for a soft fool."

Nithrin walked back into the forest with a straight spine

and an easy, fluid motion. Dak trailed after her, favoring one foot. His ankle, Rintu saw, was badly swollen.

"Suri should look at that," Rintu said. "One of her poultices might help."

"Not you too!" Boroni gave Rintu a look of contempt and left him abruptly, melting into the shade of the first trees.

Rintu caught up with Dak and Nithrin. "Does it hurt?" He probed Dak's ankle and was answered with a yelp of pain. "Come with me," he said. "There is someone who can help you. Our healer."

"Hee-ler?" Dak looked puzzled, but he went with Rintu. Nithrin left them when she came to Marek's trail, and once she was out of sight Rintu hoisted Dak onto his back.

Suri's house was almost beyond the marked limits of the village. Rintu delivered Dak and left him, too hungry to wait to see what Suri did.

It seemed that lately most of his waking hours were spent foraging, tramping miles of trails and never really filling his stomach. It was no life, he thought bitterly, remembering that time when he had first landed and had not needed to search beyond his own grove.

He found no muscales. Bigsun shone bravely over the pond, but unless its partner grew stronger soon, Rintu doubted that the stunted vines would be bearing at all. Still hungry, he started up another trail.

3

Smallsun disappeared altogether after the worst warm season in memory. Lors and Krull traveled two days down the coast and found a healthy patch of seagreens in a protected cove, but it was a long journey for regular foraging and the tribe could not be moved. They lived where they were: where their eggs were laid and where the swimmers came ashore.

They had to range farther for forest food, too—into the fastnesses of the hairy ones, the shureks. Dak was slain there before he had grown to full size.

Rintu helped carry the torn body out of the forest; six bearers for such a light burden. The new landling had still possessed the mind of a swimmer, Rintu thought. They had given him the name of a trailmaker and forced him into that role, but he had been no true Dak; he had run with his limping gait into the unblazed wilds as if it were play.

They left the body on the beach, for the skyhunters. They should have swum it to the rocks, but none of the bearers cared to brave the icy waves. Lors sang the deathsong hastily and they fled back to the village, to the dismantling of the house that Dak had barely finished.

For a while there was no more hunting, but Marek finally led a party that brought back a twin-horn. There was feasting for a day, and then more hunger.

Pellen's nameday mating turned out to be fruitful, and she laid a clutch of eggs in the birthpool. So did Mim the potter and several other females, more perhaps than usual. Neither Pellen nor any of the others gave a thought to their spawn once they were rid of it, but Rintu wondered how the ocean would receive any hatchlings that swam through the channel. So far Roko and his group were the last new swimmers to land.

Jass completed her transformation into a bloated, flippered sea creature. She could breathe only with difficulty and had to move by humping herself along the ground, but still she delayed entering the water.

No one wanted to come near her, she was so snarly. The newest landlings especially regarded her with aversion, and Rintu came upon Cuma and Roko trying to drive her toward the beach by throwing sticks.

"She has to go," they insisted when Rintu stopped them. "It isn't right for her to be here." Cuma's face bore an expression almost of pain.

Song patterns, Rintu thought; how deeply etched they were. He was offended by Jass, too, and though he understood her dilemma he could not refrain from shouting at her.

Finally, driven by jeers and even threats, the old one dragged herself into the sea.

Her body was washed up four days later.

One who profited was the small outcast, who had somehow managed to keep herself alive, and who had continued to be a special target of Jass's vituperation. Before her final change Jass had even harangued Lors until he organized hunts for the "abomination," but the quarry had always escaped. Rintu had caught occasional glimpses of her lurking around the outskirts of the settlement, but she stayed well away from the houses.

What he had seen was not prepossessing—a scabby face and a raggedly growing crest—but he couldn't help feeling a grudging admiration for her toughness. After Jass's rites he circled wide around the village, half hoping to come upon her.

He did not need to search far. Just beyond the pond she stepped from behind a stand of saplings, looking wild as a shurek. "Rintu," she said with a clarity that took him by surprise.

She moved back into the cover, and he followed. "How do you know my name?" he asked. "How do you know words at all?"

"I watch the others. I listen."

The skin on her face was healed, though scarred in places, and her body, what he could see of it through the smelly, uncured furs, did not appear malnourished. She had the half-formed crest of a maturing female, though in stature she was still far below normal.

She grinned at his stare—crookedly, because of a scar pucker on one side of her mouth. "I am a true landling. See." She waggled her fingers and thrust out her feet for his inspection. "All I lack is a name. You helped me before, Rintu." Her voice lingered over the sounds. "Now that the screaming old one is gone, I would be one of you, one of the tribe. Can you give me a name?"

He was taken aback again. "I don't know," he stammered. "Maybe. . . . Yes . . . I suppose I could do it, but it might not be accepted without a ceremony."

"I don't care. Give me one. Now."

Her gaze was insistent. Her eyes were narrow and deep-set, white slits with centers of intense green. Rintu studied her and thought of everything he knew about her. "Embri," he finally said.

"What does it mean?"

"The embri is a stringy waterweed that grows on the rocks, where nothing else will root."

"Yes, I have seen it." She cocked her head, and the unscarred corner of her mouth turned up. "And your name. What does it mean?"

He returned her smile. "The rintu is a tree that has food nuts and thick leaves that we use for roofing. If you come into the tribe and build a house, I will weave your roof for you. It is my trade."

"I would like to have a house, and a roof. I think you are well named, too."

Embri would be a strong new landling, Rintu thought, for all her diminutive size. With a bath and proper clothing, she might even be halfway presentable. "I hope they take you in," he said. "I'll speak to Lors right away."

He did, though he dared not press too hard.

Lors scratched his neck, thinking. "Is she still so small?"

"Yes, but she is healthy and will grow." Rintu tried to gauge the headman's mood. "We need more in the tribe," he ventured. "And Jass's hatred was ill-founded."

Lors scratched some more, and nodded. "Yes, Jass was crazed by her change. This . . . Embri . . . has proven herself. Bring her to me and I will give her the mark."

No one welcomed Embri, but neither did they throw sticks. Gradually, the tribe accepted her. She was eager to learn all their ways and she never came back empty-handed from foraging. She willingly joined hunts, too. Marek was amazed by her skill with a spear and Boroni by her cleverness in devising snares. If anything, she tried to do too much for someone with the name of a waterweed, but who would object when she was so generous in sharing?

The complaints came slowly at first, but they were persistent.

Her eating habits disgusted everyone who knew of them. Treeworts, grubs and even diggers—no fit food for a landling. "But I see many of you hungry," she said when Rintu tried to remonstrate.

Her house was a joke. It wasn't even properly attached to its tree, but mushroomed upward from a leg-deep hole. She had slept in burrows in the forest and kept warm, she insisted.

Rintu purposely forgot his promise to help with the roof. Embri built it herself, and when he sneaked by to look he saw a ridiculous thatch of moss and branches and miss-matched leaves. It was sure to leak in a storm, he knew; perhaps it would even collapse.

The waterweed female's worst fault, though, was her in-cessant talk. The forest should have taught her silence, Rintu thought, but it seemed to have had the opposite effect. She questioned everyone about everything—matings, egg-laying, the shureks, what they remembered of the waterlife. Things no one else discussed.

She mortified Pellen by actually inspecting the birthpool and reporting that there were no eggs or hatchlings in it. She angered Marek by suggesting that the shureks could be driven away; even claiming (though no one believed her) to have killed one. Lors she offended by asking why the tribal mark was necessary when there were no other landlings.

"But why, what *is* the reason?" she persisted when Rintu came to scold her for the insult to the headman.

"It does not matter; we do not question custom," he said sternly. Actually, he had heard tales of other tribes of land-lings on the coast, but no one he knew had ever seen them. It was no concern of Embri's, however. She had to learn to control her curiosity and her tongue or she would be an out-cast again.

"What else have I done wrong?" Embri asked. They were sitting beneath Embri's house tree on a day of rare sunshine, she plaiting a basket while Rintu lectured. Embri was always busy, her hands as nimble as her tongue. She had improved somewhat in appearance—at least she was now clean and wore properly cured hides—but Rintu feared that she would always be ugly. Her crest had come in dull and uneven, and she still had in her eyes the untamed look of a forest crea-ture.

"One other thing," he said. "You must not ask questions about the waterlife. It belongs to a time when we were . . . less than landlings, and no one likes to talk about it."

"You are ashamed?"

"No, not exactly that. It's just that this is our life now. Remember how Jass hated you and the other ungrown swimmers? I think you brought it to her mind that she was about to go back. Now, with the ocean so cold, no one wants to think of beginnings or endings."

"I understand." Embri moved closer to him without pausing in her work. "You don't mind talking about it to me, though, do you?" She gave him no time to answer. "Do you remember how it was when you began to lose your waterskin and the old ones sang their landsongs?"

He nodded.

"Well, to me there weren't many songs because I changed so soon and so fast. That's why I have to find out everything now for myself. And why I don't seem to understand about custom."

"But you must, or everyone will avoid you. You will become another Jass."

The warning had effect, but not for long. Soon she was back to prying again, chattering to Roko about her own way of drying hides until he chased her away.

When Rintu saw it, he cringed. She was such an embarrassment, and he had sponsored her.

Nithrin, by contrast, was shy and quiet, and fulfilled her name by becoming more beautiful every day. Her flaming crest was fully extended, and when she walked under Bigsun her head was surrounded by a gleaming corona. She had the finest house of any of the newcomers, though she had no skill in building, and more cooking pots than anyone in the village.

Rintu had woven her roof with special care, taking a full day. Like most of the males in the tribe, he eagerly awaited her first mating. It was difficult, however, to predict when a female's heat would come, and aside from following Nithrin constantly there was nothing he could do to assure that he would be in the vicinity at the right time.

He wasn't. He was digging for marsh tubers up at the high spring when Embri came rushing upon him like a stormwind. "Come with me—now—or they will kill each other!" She pushed him when he did not respond fast enough, and he almost fell into the mud.

She steadied him, but continued to urge: "Marek and Boroni. They're fighting for Nithrin, and they're *wild*. You've got to stop them."

He shook her off, his disappointment exploding in a sharp laugh. "So that's all! What do you expect them to do—clasp hands and cast lots?"

She stamped her foot, slipping and miring herself to the knee. "Do you think I'm stupid? I've seen mating fights, but I tell you this is different. They've been at it since high sun, and neither will give up." She extricated herself and swiped angrily at her muddy leg. "I thought they were your friends!"

"Where are they?" It wouldn't hurt to take a look, he decided. It just might be serious, for someone like Nithrin.

"Nithrin's house. And hurry."

Infected by Embri's distress, Rintu ran down the entire trail and arrived panting at Nithrin's tree space.

Marek and Boroni circled each other, naked except for loin wraps. They moved with the heaviness of exhaustion, and their labored gasps, when they grappled, seemed torn from their bodies.

Nithrin crouched in her doorway, her eyes wide as lim shells. She looked at Embri and Rintu with no sign of recognition.

Embri held Rintu by the arm. "Don't go near her. You must keep your head and stop them."

He shook her off, though he had no intention of approaching Nithrin. To catch her scent and enter the fray himself, so late, would be a gross misconduct.

But so would it be to interfere. Marek and Boroni rolled and thrashed, their films of sweat making purchase difficult. Marek obtained a choke hold and pressed until Boroni's eyes bulged, but the bigger male dug his heels into the earth and heaved.

Boroni was on top, and Rintu saw that his greater strength would prevail. Marek still pressed murderously with his thumbs, but Boroni began to pound the hunter's head until Marek loosened his grip.

In any usual contest Marek would have made the sign of surrender, but his eyes were wild with desperation. He reached into his wrap and drew out a knife.

Embri screamed, and Rintu stepped forward.

He was too late. Marek buried the knife in Boroni's side, and Boroni collapsed. Marek pushed the heavy body aside and staggered to his feet, his face masklike in the grip of his fever.

He saw Rintu, and the mask slipped. "Get him to Suri. I . . ."

Nithrin stood up and he went to her, into the hut, without a backward glance.

"Help me," Rintu said to Embri. He pulled the knife from Boroni's side, just below the fin ridge. Blood welled out, and he slapped on his own belt pouch for a compress.

Embri tied the belt tightly about Boroni's body. "Do you think we can carry him?" She looked dubiously at the huge, inert form.

"No, we can drag him. I'll make something." Rintu hastily fashioned a travois from his own cloak and two poles raided from Nithrin's roof. He and Embri rolled Boroni onto it.

The wounded male cried out, and Embri adjusted his bandage. She took one pole and Rintu the other.

Embri was uncharacteristically quiet all the way to the healer's hut, and Rintu was grateful. Boroni looked bad. If he died, Rintu knew, Marek could be exiled. In any case, the use of a weapon in a mating fight was a grave offense.

Boroni groaned each time the travois bumped, and his bandage was soaked with blood when they arrived at Suri's hut. The tall healer took him inside and dropped her door-flap.

Embri turned to Rintu and exploded. "It's so stupid, so needless! Why should Marek have had to fight for Nithrin? Everyone knows she prefers him to anyone else, and his feelings are no secret. Why did this happen?"

"Marek shouldn't have used a knife."

She made a gesture of impatience. "I know that. It's not what I meant. Why should they fight at all?"

"It is the way. Marek's and Nithrin's feelings—they have nothing to do with mating. It is not something you can control."

"So I've been told. But all the same, I plan to pick *my* partner."

"Hah! You'll see when your time comes. You'll go with whoever is nearest, or whoever wins, if there are several. You might think otherwise now, just as I thought often of Nithrin and of how it might be with her. But when you have the fever there is no thinking, none at all, just your need."

"I will be different," she continued to insist.

Rintu turned his back. It was nothing to talk about, and she never knew when to stop. Her voice went on, but he didn't listen, thinking only of Boroni and Marek and of what might happen.

Suri came to her door. "He will live," she said.

4

Boroni recovered, but Marek lost much of his standing in the tribe. It would have been worse for him if he had not been their best hunter, but the cold continued and so did the need for hides and what meat they could get. Embri flourished on fungi and grubs while klava dulled the pangs of hunger for the others. What should have been the warm season came and went, with the tribe still in their furs. There was only one landing, and the few swimmers who made it to shore were so hopelessly immature that they were all left on the beach. "Let them do as Embri did," Lors decreed. "If any survive, then we can have a naming ceremony."

"Maybe." Others were unsure even of that. The squirmy creatures with their half-formed limbs looked nothing like landlings. Pellen made a grimace of disgust when she saw them. "Are we to become like shureks, saddled with mewling young? We are not *animals*!"

There was no food in the near woods, though the swimmer-landlings somehow dragged themselves that far. Rintu suspected that Embri carried them from the beach at night and perhaps even fed them, but it was not enough. One by one the bodies were found in the forest.

Pellen and some of the other females were angry that the malformed ones had survived even that little while. Rintu followed them when they confronted Embri. He wished he could stop feeling responsible for her actions, but he had named her and that he could not undo.

"They died, then?" Embri twisted her hands as she faced her accusers. They had surprised her as she was leaving her house.

"Yes, to the last one." Pellen's eyes were as coldly hard as sea rocks. "They were not fit, and we are all glad. You see, it did no good for you to go against our wishes and help them."

Rintu stepped forward. "No one knows who . . ."

Someone made a rude sound, and suddenly he was finished with defending Embri. She knew what she did, and would have to face the consequences. He shrugged and walked away.

"Come back here!" Embri shouted.

He froze in his tracks.

Embri stood bent, trembling with anger. "Of course I helped them!" She turned from him to Pellen with clenched fists. "You call yourselves landlings, you and your tribe. You say you are not animals, to take care of your young. Well, perish then, like the superior beings you are. Perish in your pride and in your slavish customs, while the shureks take over the land and the killerfish the seas. Tell me Pellen, Nithrin: why do you bother to lay your eggs at all?"

Rintu was as stunned as the females. Tears coursed down Embri's darkly mottled face. She raked her crest with her fingers and gave a final despairing cry before she ran off in the direction of the beach.

Rintu waited for an hour before he went looking for her. She was mad, he thought, and not to be held accountable. Perhaps it was her strange diet. Most disquieting, though— he had to admit it—her rantings had contained grains of truth.

He found her in the dunes, stretched out on her back. She seemed calmer, but her face was still suffused with emotion and her eyes were curiously unfocused.

He knew the reason as soon as he came near and she raised her fur—her sex was fully opened and glistening. She was the last female he would have desired, but the smell of her musk drove away any scruples; he closed his eyes and pretended she was Nithrin.

After the mating, Rintu avoided her, and Embri finally left him alone. She spent most of her time away from the village, and it was just as well; there was talk that she was the cause of the tribe's continuing bad fortune.

Marek's latest hunting party returned empty-handed, with four able tribe members torn by the teeth of shureks. Three did not recover. The ground hardened with cold and the fruitvines died, and even gourds and tubers became scarce. Krull and two others went into the final change, but without the layers of insulating fat beneath their waterskins they did not survive in the ocean even as long as Jass. Were there any old ones left in the sea? Rintu wondered.

He walked along the beach, searching for signs: drifting patches of green or surfacing spouts.

"No, there is nothing out there." Embri, shivering in wet furs, came up to him from behind.

He didn't question how she knew his thoughts; concern over the last deaths was general. But she had seemed so positive. "How do you know?" He looked at her again. She couldn't have swum out; no one could any longer venture beyond the shallows.

She was wet only from the waist, however. Probably digging in the dead seagreen bed, he thought.

"Those last swimmers," she said. "I tried to sing to them, as the old ones did to us, but there was nothing to reach. They knew less even than I when I landed. I think they had not been taught at all."

"Then how could they have lived in the water as long as they did?"

She shrugged. "I think there will be no more landings." She hugged herself and danced her feet up and down, but she seemed reluctant to leave.

"Go home and get warm," Rintu said. He was angry with her again; it always happened. "There was no reason for you to look for greens; we all know they are gone. Why do you persist in acting so foolishly?"

She lifted her head and met his gaze. "I wasn't looking for greens; I was at the birthpool. I have been thinking about it, and I decided what to do. I have closed it up with rocks."

He stared at her, unable to believe such wild talk. The pool was the size of two houses, and deep. No one person could fill it in.

Her hands, though, were raw and bleeding. "No pool— why, they will kill you," he said.

"No, no, you don't understand!" She pulled at his arm and laughed. "I mean, I closed up the little channel, the opening, so no more eggs and hatchlings will be swept out into the ocean. Maybe in the pool they'll have a chance to grow."

She stood on one foot like a runty longbill, looking inordinately pleased with herself. Rintu experienced a wave of helplessness. What could he say to her? Undoubtedly she meant well, but she was so misguided. She had no sense of rightness, of custom, of the way of life—she had said it herself.

Hatchlings had to go to sea, to become swimmers, even if it meant their death. The thought of hatchlings growing in the birthpool, becomeing swimmers there, was abhorrent. No landlings would ever suffer such a perversion.

She chattered on. "We could feed them, in the pool. We could take the place of the old ones. We could—"

"Stop!" he thundered. He seized her shoulder. He had meant to shake her, but she felt so frail, even through the fur, that he checked himself. "No one will permit it," he said more calmly. "They will drive you out if they see what you have done. You must remove the barrier now." He pushed her toward the rocks at the end of the beach.

She tore herself from his grasp. "Never! I won't lose my eggs like all the others. What do I care if I am an outcast again? The village is dead anyway, if you go on as you are now."

He reached out to slap her. It was monstrous, to talk about "my" eggs, and to want to cling to them. It was disgusting, and he was the one who had bred with her.

She escaped, twisting her ugly scarred face into a snarl before she ran into the dunes.

Rintu climbed over the rocks and looked across the marsh to the birthpool. He imagined fat, thick-skinned, flippered swimmers thrashing about in it. Gross creatures with landling faces. With his face.

He groaned. It would be a shame beyond measure, but he would not let it happen. Embri would not be laying her eggs for some weeks, he figured, as he counted on his fingers. He would guarantee that the sea channel was open and stayed open if he had to stand guard every day.

The tide was out, and he was able to cross the sandflats behind the marshes with dry feet. At the birthpool, though, he had to wade in the icy water to heave out one by one the stones that Embri had piled into a dam.

It took him until nightfall. He straightened up with an aching back and legs that were too numb to feel more pain. As he looked out to sea, the winds seemed to rest for a moment and the surface of the water calmed, as if thanking him for his labors, and became luminous from the sinking sun. He watched the ripples turn from silver to gold to streaky fire, and he felt a warming sense of peace. Smallsun might return, but even if it didn't and the tribe were to die out, it would be done with dignity, as befitted true landlings.

Embri did not attempt to rebuild the dam. She was ill for many days; a chill, Suri said, and a weakness from eggs early-lost.

Rintu was vastly relieved and determined to keep a safe distance from her in the future. It was an easy resolve, as there was little activity of any kind in the settlement. When the rain froze, falling white on the ground, the villagers were too terrified to leave their houses. They kept fires burning continuously indoors, though there was little to cook. Rintu lived on his store of nuts and what greens he could find, and slept a great deal.

Embri made light of his defenses by coming to him at night, and though he took her, it was with shame. She should have known—she did know—that it was degrading to repeatedly seek out the same partner. Marek had tried it with Nithrin, and had lost even more of his stature. Rintu feared for his own name, and he did not even have the sweetness of Marek's reward.

At least, Rintu thought the next morning, no one knew of their folly. Embri left his house in the darkness, though she had lain in his arms for some time after her heat was done.

5

The days of Bigsun finally lengthened and the forest gave food again, but without Smallsun there were no long-days of continuous light. Rintu remembered Krull's story, that Smallsun had once been gone for the forty cycles of a land-life. A dire prospect, he thought, yet if that had happened, some of the tribe must have survived.

Rintu began to forget that the sky had once been brighter. The cheerless forest was his world now. He and Roko went down the coast after seagreens, and on the open beaches it was still bone-chilling cold.

The new seagreen bed continued to bear, however, and the two males carried home heavy packs. Lors declared a feast; not the namefeast it should have been, but a farewell for him. The headman had begun his change, which they all now knew was no longer a final stage but a death sign.

Lors did not pass on the white cape, as everyone had expected. "There is yet time," he said, but Rintu suspected that he could not make a choice. It would be left to a contest, and with Marek in disgrace anyone might prevail.

Embri did not come to the feast. Rintu had not seen her since the wintry night of their last mating, and he did not ask after her. He had repaired the roofs of nearly every house in the village, but though hers was badly caved in she had not asked for his help.

She did not even claim her share of greens. After the feast, his judgment dulled by klava, Rintu gave in to his nagging concern.

Her squat house was empty. It was damp and infested with woodcrawlers, the fire pit cold.

Cuma, who had the nearest house, knew little. "I thought she was on a hunt, though why she would go alone. . . . But you know, she has always been strange."

"Did you see her leave?" Rintu asked. "How long has it been?"

"Many days." She held up both hands. "Maybe twice this long. Before that, though, I seldom saw her at home. I don't know where she went, but last time she had a big pack."

So she had gone back to the forest, then. Perhaps it was best, he thought.

"Yes, very strange," Cuma continued. "Especially when she was so near her eggtime."

The klava left Rintu's head in a rush. Would she dare again? He left Cuma standing with an open mouth as he raced off to the shore.

The birthpool was undisturbed. It was also empty, though half the females in the tribe had visited it in recent weeks.

Rintu crouched low and peered again, searching for the cloudy clusters of eggs that should have been attached to the sides and bottom.

He saw nothing but a few strands of membrane that whipped in the current. Outside the pool, the ocean churned wild and deadly.

Embri would never have accepted such a fate for her eggs. Filled with new fears, Rintu began to track her down.

Marek had seen her some time ago on the highest trail, and Rintu followed it to its end at the seeping spring. The mud around the pool was recently trampled, but there was no sign of a camp. If Embri had been there for sweet water, she had obtained it and left.

He tried to think as she would. She would need fresh water for herself, but for eggs or hatchlings she had to have water from the ocean.

He turned toward the coast again.

She would not go south and chance discovery by seagreen gatherers. The coast north of them was a tortuous terrain of cliffs and gullies and rocky coves, but he did not have to travel far before he found her.

She had made a campsite on a narrow strip of sandy beach, sheltered between great standing rocks. Rintu stayed out of sight, scanning the area. About a tree length from the tent and the pile of firewood, he found what he sought.

Embri had made her own basin at the tideline, digging to water and lining the pool with stones. She slept at the lower rim of the pool, as if guarding it or its contents from the incoming waves.

Rintu felt a churning in the pit of his stomach. But when he thought of the other pool, the empty one, he could not bring himself to rush out as a destroyer.

He waited at the nearest of the rock towers, and when Embri awoke he moved behind it. He watched through a narrow fissure as she opened the pool briefly to the tide, closed it again and kept watch until the waves receded. She cooked something for herself at an open fire pit on the dry sand, then dropped her furs to wade about in the shallows between the far rocks, where he lost sight of her.

She returned with dripping handfuls of something green. When she fed them to whatever was in the pool, Rintu felt another wave of nausea.

Still, he did not act. Embri's attitude, as she bent over the pool, was something he had never seen. He would have to talk to her, he decided, before he fixed on what to do. He would have to look at what was in the pool.

Embri was tying on her furs when he showed himself. She screamed and reached into the tent, pulling out a short-handled spear.

Her face was tight-lipped and grim. "Stay back." She brandished the weapon, and Rintu stopped.

He held out his hands. "I mean no harm." He tried to speak softly, to allay her fears. "Let me see what you have done. It concerns me. It concerns all of us. We should talk, as landlings and as friends."

"You mean it—as a friend?" Her mouth relaxed a bit, and she lowered the spear. She looked haggard, on the edge of exhaustion.

He made the sign of truth, and it was no pretense. He felt no more anger toward her, but a kind of awe.

"Then come and look." She still held the spear as they walked to the pool. He knelt at the rim and she stood over him, watching him warily.

A single hatchling lazily circled the pool. It was the length of his two hands and the breadth of one, with well-grown flipper and fin extensions. Rintu could discern the landling form and even something of the facial features beneath the waterskin. He felt the sweat on his own face, but to his surprise he was not as repulsed as he had expected.

"The others all died," Embri said. "The tide took most of the eggs, and those that hatched wouldn't feed. Except this one. It eats, and grows every day. Already the pool is too small." There was pride in her voice. "See, it knows me." She put down her spear and knelt beside Rintu, and the creature swam to her.

She lifted it out of the water.

"Don't do that!" he cried. "It can't breathe!"

The gill slits of the hatchling opened and closed furiously. Embri put her mouth on the creature's mouth and blew, and the thrashing stopped. Rintu saw the narrow chest expanding, and he remembered when he was a swimmer and his water-breathers had closed; how he had been forced to surface for gasps of air.

Embri raised her head. "It is learning," she said. "If I help, it can stay out for minutes at a time." She looked down at the hatchling with the peculiar expression he had noted before, and it seemed to Rintu that she was less ugly than he remembered.

She replaced the hatchling in the water, where it swam on its back, watching them.

"Yes, the pool is much too small," Rintu said.

"I have started digging another one." Embri pointed to a ragged hole just beyond her camp. "It goes slowly, though; I don't dare to leave the hatchling for long." She started to say something else, but stopped. The unspoken question remained in her eyes.

He backed away, affronted at first and then afraid. Did she really expect him to stay and help her? He didn't think so badly now of her saving the hatchling. It even seemed right for her. But he could never in his wildest projections conceive of playing a personal part in such an undertaking.

Still, there was the fear, as if he could no longer trust himself. "I must be getting back," he said. "It will be dark soon, and the cliffs are treacherous."

"Of course." She stroked the hatchling with her hand and did not look up when he left.

He returned after four handspans of days, concerned about the night frosts which had already begun. Visions of a small dead waterform haunted him as he struggled up and down the ravines, and he was unable to convince himself that it might be for the best.

Embri came to meet him with the hatchling, wrapped in a damp mossblanket, in her arms. "How does it do?" he asked. He kept himself from looking down at her burden.

She held it out.

The hatchling appeared shrunken at first, but then he saw that it was actually longer, though it had lost most of its insulating fat. Only a thin layer of membrane covered the landling face, and on its now recognizable arms and legs the waterskin was cracked and beginning to peel.

"But it isn't even swimmer sized!" Rintu blurted, shocked. He turned to Embri. "This is what comes of keeping it so much out of the water. Didn't I tell you—"

She ignored his rating. "It has to be living outside before the next bad season starts. In the water it would die." She bent over the hatchling to help it breathe, then started toward the camp.

The new pool was finished. Embri stood beside it, with the hatchling still in her arms. "It still swims in there sometimes, but already I think it feels the cold." She tested the water with her foot, shivered and turned away. She carried her bundle into the tent.

There was barely squatting room inside for the two adults. Embri put down the hatchling and oiled a bit of its exposed newskin.

The creature was so impossibly small and helpless, Rintu thought. And Embri was so thin. How could she keep the hatchling and herself alive in this place? The only provisions he could see in the tent were a few stringy tubers.

He shared his own rations with her and she ate greedily, feeding the hatchling from her own mouth. Soon it slept.

"Can you bring me more food?" She looked down at her hands, twisting them. "I can't hunt, you see. It needs me, at times, to breathe, and I have to stay close."

Rintu had his own shame, for either to agree or to refuse would be a dishonor. "It is a hard journey, and will get worse," he finally said, temporizing.

"Yes, but..." She traced circles with her fingers on the floor hide. "Nobody would need to know where you were going."

She understood, then, his real concern—that someone would discover his secret. Boroni, who still looked to be headman, or Marek, who might regain face by exposing a more flagrant offense.

No, he thought, it would be better for her to return to the village where she had a warm house and access to the forest, and where he could help her covertly without being absent for suspicious periods.

He suggested it, and she reacted with confusion. "But what will they do to me? What will they do to the hatchling?

You said once that they would kill me for interfering with the births."

"I spoke rashly, in anger. I was overly concerned with the shame. You know we don't usually harm one another."

She started to speak, and he held up his hand. "Not even in mating battles. That . . . between Marek and Boroni . . . was unusual."

"Perhaps, but what about Jass when I landed? She was ready to crush my head."

He was silent for a long moment. "I thought differently then, too. We didn't know that there would be no more swimmers in the ocean. Now everyone believes there will be no more landings."

She shook her head, unconvinced, and he continued to argue. "The worst they will do is avoid you until they understand what you and the hatchling mean to them. Then they might even give you a new name."

"The animal?" she suggested sourly.

He squeezed her hand and tried to make her smile. "No, someone will make up a new word. One that means 'the female who keeps her young.' That is all that will happen."

She still frowned, but she did not remove her hand. "You will come with me; stay with me?"

He jerked away. She hadn't changed, he thought; she still asked too much.

Outside, curled in his cloak, he forgave her. If she had a mind that worked like that of others, she would not now be sleeping with the hatchling. He would help her back, her and the hatchling, in the morning, but he would not enter the village with them. He would speak up for her later, if any wanted to cast her out, but what she had asked for could not be considered.

It was a slow and difficult journey, with Embri encumbered with the hatchling, but yet Rintu was oddly sorry when they arrived at their own beach. It was late afternoon, and they stopped in the dunes.

The hatchling had stood the journey well, and showed no distress at being out of the water so long. Rintu had thought to make another pool, a hidden one, but they decided it was not necessary.

He began to think his plan would work. "I'll go into the village first," he said. "You wait until dark, then slip in quietly with the hatchling. With luck, no one will notice you."

Embri settled into a hollow of webgrass, clutching the hatchling more tightly than was necessary.

He had difficulty with his voice as he continued: "You can show yourself in the morning, but keep the hatchling inside as long as you can. Until it has a better form. I'll see that you get food, but no one must know."

She nodded, but he could see her chin trembling.

Now don't spoil it, he felt like shouting. You will, I know it; you'll give me away.

He said nothing, however, but turned from them brusquely and half ran toward the forest.

At the first trees he turned and looked back. Even then he thought he could leave them, but when she stood and started toward him he did not wave her back.

He heard the horrified whispers already, and the jeers, but they did not seem important. What crowded his mind was a plan for the new house he would have to build. He waited until Embri and the hatchling joined him, and they walked into the village together.

Part II

THE RED FLOWER

1

Nithrin caught her foot on an exposed root as she stumbled into the forest. Too exhausted to recover her balance, she sprawled full length.

The wet humus cushioned what could have been a bad fall. When she had determined that she was unhurt, she relaxed into a softness that felt blissfully warm compared to the icy waters of the birthpool. She pulled her cloak close around her and lay for some time while the ache in her loins subsided.

Well, it was done, she thought. Marek could glower and rave, but once again she had foiled him. She felt no triumph, though; not this time. Only dread of the scene to come. The deceptive warmth began to leave her, and she shivered.

It was the damp, which had seeped through her summer furs. She sat up and tried to brush herself off, but discovered with dismay that the front of her wrap bore a huge muddy stain. She scrubbed at it with raw knuckles, ineffectually. It would never come clean, she knew. Her eyes stung with tears, and she clamped her teeth to keep from blubbering.

She would have liked to howl—a despairing protest against the ruined garment and the frigid birthpool; against Marek and against the unfairness of squatting in numb agony while her guts had cramped and heaved and spewed out a clump of eggs that were doomed as soon as they left her body. Not that she cared about the eggs—she was no Embri or Suri to dote on such—but she did care about Marek, and feared what he would do when he discovered that she had once more given her spawn to the ocean.

For ten cycles he had been pressuring her—ever since Embri and Rintu had saved first one hatchling and then two others—and finally she had halfway promised to use the new small pool in the old seagreen bed. But at the last moment she hadn't been able to do it. The thought of herself enslaved like Embri and now Suri, tied for two or three cycles to a monstrosity of a hatchling that could do nothing for itself, the orderly pattern of her days shattered. . . .

No, she had acted correctly, as a true landling, she reassured herself; as anyone in the tribe (except those few infected with Embri's madness) would verify. She had no cause for guilt, or for fear of Marek, headman though he was. She gave up scraping at her fur—perhaps when it was dry it would brush out—and pushed herself to her feet. Her inner thighs were sticky with seeping residue, and she needed to wash. Perhaps, if the water at the pond was warm enough, she could even have a real soak.

Nithrin followed a wide trail between the thick-trunked trees. The forest wore its milder aspect, green and leafy overhead and comparatively dry underfoot. The memory of winter persisted, though, in the fallen branches over which she had to climb and in the scoured bark of many of the giants.

She kept to the trail, though a shortcut would have saved her half an hour. The fleshy vines that had formed the undergrowth in the time of both suns had been succeeded by thorny brambles daunting to one with bare legs. Nithrin's skin was smooth and unmarked, a tribute to her care.

The trail descended to an open meadow where the fresh-water pond nestled in a circlet of reeds and muscales. Nithrin waded through the stiff, tall grass that brushed wetly against her legs, raising her fur to protect its hem. At the edge of the muscale thicket, she parted the bushes carefully and slipped through to the water.

She tested it and gasped. Still winter-cold. She managed a squat-bath in the shallows, surrounded by the blossomless tendrils of her name flower, and even that was hard to endure.

On the bank, rubbing herself dry with a handful of moss, she leaned over the water and studied her wavery reflection. Every time she did so she expected to see a change— a dulling of her crest or a stoop to her back—as she had noticed in so many of her fellows. The brief summers and long, harsh winters had told markedly on most of them, especially the females, though even Marek's face had become more deeply lined of late.

But Nithrin appeared to herself the same as always. A perfect crest and smooth limbs glistened in the water, and she smiled in relief. She peered closer, to see a face that she had been told often enough was beautiful. She supposed it must be, and was immeasurably grateful for the gift. So grateful that it went beyond vanity.

Her physical perfection was the only security she knew. Without it, she hardly dared think of what she would do, of what the tribe might think of her for the ways they could not see in which she was so unlike others. Even as she was now reassured of her safety by the evidence of her eyes, the question arose, as it always did: *What if they knew?*

The Nithrin who had so much to hide stared out of the water with frightened eyes as ripples distorted the reflected lines of her body. Before she could look away she had become first an elongated ogre and then a misshapen cripple. She put her hands to her eyes and stepped backward, but the spell was on her and she could not escape. The light came even through her clamped fingers: the light that at unpredictable times would tear at her eyes until it seemed that something dropped from them and she could see what no one else could: things that should have remained safely covered.

When she removed her hands and opened her eyes, the water was transparent, revealing every rotted stick and every clump of mollusks on the muddy bottom. She jerked her gaze away, to the overhanging fronds of muscales, each spidery inner fiber as clear as the outer pattern on the leaves. When she looked down she could follow the roots of the shrubs as they angled away from the pond, and even deeper as she probed, through layers of clay and rock, until she cried out in fear of what she might find and sank to the earth.

She ground her fists into her eyes, and the light became a searing pain. Still, it was better than the seeing, and she persisted until unconsciousness blotted out everything.

She heard Cuma's voice as though through layers of sleep. "Nithrin, what is it? Are you hurt?" She heard sucking footsteps and the sound of someone crashing through the muscales, and barely had time to pull herself out of her trance.

She pretended to be crying, and soon it was no pretense. Cuma knelt beside her and placed a hesitant hand on her heaving shoulders. "Did you get a cramp from the water? You feel so cold."

"No, no," Nithrin hiccuped. She lifted her head to peer through slitted fingers.

Her vision was normal again. The leaves hung decently impenetrable, and below them Cuma's pointed face was puckered with worry.

"I just came from the birthpool," Nithrin said. "It was especially bad this time."

Compassion replaced Cuma's frown. She picked up Nirthrin's fur. "Here, wrap up and warm yourself." She chafed the cold hands. "Let's move where it's dry." She led Nithrin through the muscales to a knoll raised above the waving grass. They sat close, both with faces turned to the faint rays of the sun.

Cuma continued to fuss, and Nithrin let her. It was no disgrace to have a physical weakness. But the other. . . .

She had found out early that no one else shared her inner sight. When it had first come she was not long matured, and she had not known it was unusual. But as soon as she saw the shock and the fear engendered by her "spells," she had learned to hide them. No one knew the true extent of her power—that when it came she could see into trees, and if she were with someone she could see their bones and the foodsacs and the airsacs and even the tracery of tubes that carried the blood.

Nithrin was determined that no one would ever know. She admitted to being a "finder" (for there had been others, in the old stories), and would sometimes locate a lost knife or a sewing prick or an ornament. Once she had indicated to Boroni where he could find hardstone for spear tips, but he had asked so many questions that she had never done it again.

Cuma talked on, offering comfort. "Would you like to see Suri? She made a brew for me once that helped with the afterpains. I'll go with you to her house."

"That one?" Nithrin's bitterness returned, sharpening her voice. "Is she ever at home now that she's raising one of *those* in Embri's pool?"

Cuma blinked. "I forgot. I still can't believe she's done it." She glanced at Nithrin and away again before she continued. "Marek has been after me about it, too. All of us. Wasn't it difficult for you?"

Nithrin straightened her spine. "To hold out against him? No, it wasn't hard. I could never bring myself to go against nature that way. Against the teachings. Never. Everyone knows it's wrong. Whenever I think of that second one of Embri's. . . ."

"I know. I don't like to see that fish girl among us, either. She makes me feel sick. But Rowan turned out all right, you'll have to admit. He looks like any other landling."

"Looks, yes. But who knows what goes on in his head, with no teachers but those two crazy ones."

Cuma nodded. "I'm not surprised at Embri trying it again and again, but Suri. . . ."

"She's not like us, either. Perhaps being a healer has changed her somehow. Those herbs and potions. . . ." Nithrin's smooth brow furrowed. "It's Embri's fault, though. Hers and Rintu's. I don't understand why Marek listens to them. Why he protects them. If it weren't for him, they would have been driven out long ago." Her crest rustled as she shook her head in perplexity. "What is happening to the patterns we were all taught? Surely the old ones knew when they sang. . . ."

Cuma shifted uncomfortably, and Nithrin recalled herself. How had she gotten on such a topic? She recognized that she was still not in control, and until she was, it would be better for her to be alone. "I feel stronger now," she said. She stood and made the sign of thanks. "I can get home all right."

"Are you sure? I'll be happy to go with you."

A flood of gratitude warmed Nithrin. Cuma was a true friend, and she had so few. "No, it isn't necessary," she said, smiling. "You were looking for muscales, weren't you? You needn't bother; there aren't any ripe ones here, none at all. But if you feel like diving—if you can stand the cold. . ." She described the location of the mollusks she had seen.

Cuma's eyes widened.

"Don't ask me—just one of those hunches," Nithrin called over her shoulder as she ran.

Minutes later, she upbraided herself. Cuma would wonder, and perhaps even talk. She couldn't afford it; not if her spells were to become as uncontrollable as this last one.

Before, they had usually been a flash of light that lasted seconds; easy to conceal. And the longer ones—though she had never experienced one as extended as this—had always given warning, like a false heat, and she had had time to get away from curious eyes.

Her actual heats were another trial to her. Violent and prolonged, they were almost more an ordeal than a pleasure. No other females, she suspected, ever left their partners in exhausted sleep as she did and went out seeking a mate again. Sometimes she couldn't even remember who had mounted her.

Of course it was usually Marek, who now that he was headman cared little about breaking custom. Nithrin did, but where Marek was concerned she was weak.

She had come upon whispers—conversations that stopped when she approached. She knew what it would have been like for her if she had not been so admired for her beauty.

Her house was not far from the pond, one of a group of six that shared the same shelter of a dipu grove. The arching trunks and lacing branches of the dark conifers created a permanent gloom, but they provided protection from the worst storms of winter. The dipu throve in the harsher climate, which was fortunate; several of the larger gourd trees, once favored for houses, had died and come crashing down.

The house was the second Nithrin had had made for herself. It was sturdier than the first, double-walled and fast-chinked, with the sloping type of roof that Rintu built now to withstand the snow, and with a fire pit and chimney in the new manner devised by Rowan. Her tree space was less than she had had before, barely enough for proper seclusion, but it was something she had learned to accept. Danger from hunger-driven animals had forced them all to live closer together.

Nithrin stooped to enter, then straightened and slowly paced the five steps of the high wall, gliding her fingers over the wealth that hung there and letting it reassure her of her worth.

Her walls and floor were covered with several thicknesses of soft hides. Her clothing furs hung on the high wall and her ornaments were arrayed on the opposite low one, while her cooking and eating vessels crowded the stone around her fire pit. The furs were each different and each one perfect, with no burns or visible stains or tears in the sewing. Her bone and shell beads and bracelets and anklets appeared dull now in the dim light, but when she had a fire they gleamed from the wall in eye-pleasing patterns.

Nithrin removed the anklet she was wearing, wiped it with a scrap of hide and hung it in its place. Tired though she was, she resisted the appeal of her bed corner until she had sponged her soiled cloak. Then she rubbed her face and hands and feet with oil and surrendered to the comfort of springy moss and warm furs.

She had barely drifted into sleep when something thunked against the wall near her head. It came again and again, in a regular pattern.

It was Marek's signal, and at first she covered her ears and ignored it. She wasn't ready to face him yet, for all her certainty that she was in the right about the eggs. She didn't want a quarrel. He was misguided, yes, but still he was Marek, who had been her first friend and protector and the partner of her first heat, who was closer to her than any other landling.

And of course, he was their headman.

She made herself ready to meet him, selecting a fur the color of ocean froth that left her arms and lower legs bare, footwraps fastened with killerfish teeth, and a high, ringed bone collar. She scented her crest with crushed lupods and pushed each scale erect, then stooped low through the doorway so as not to disturb her handiwork.

Marek waited the correct distance from her tree space. Nithrin motioned for him to enter, and he came running. "Are you all right?" His face was creased with deep lines, more so than usual. "I met Cuma, and she said you were ill."

He took in her appearance. "But you must be recovered now." His expression softened into one she knew well. "I haven't seen you so beautiful since . . . since before . . ." He stiffened into wariness again.

"Come inside," Nithrin said quickly. So Cuma hadn't told him. She almost wished she had. At least, the first anger would be over now.

She motioned for him to sit, and sank to her haunches

beside him. The sinews on Marek's body stood out tight with tension. By now, she knew, he had guessed.

"So tell me," he said, "are they in the new pool?"

She refused to answer, but her defiant gaze spoke for her.

Marek was too calm. "You wouldn't do it for me, even if you care nothing for the tribe?"

She lashed out. "Don't talk to me about the tribe! I care more about it than you would ever understand. And no, I wouldn't disgrace myself so—do something so disgusting—even for you." She lifted her chin. "And certainly not for Embri and Rintu, who seem to be the ones who tell you what to think these days."

He looked away from her into the dark fire pit. His silent reproach goaded her more than anger would have done. "Ask anyone," she said. "Ask them what they would think of their headman if he started carrying a hatchling around like Rintu did; if he took it into his house. What if it turned out like the fish girl? What would everyone think of *me*?"

"Ah, there you have it," he finally said. He turned to face her, and he could have been a stranger. "What would they think of *you*? Would they forget the eyes like the sea and the smooth body and the flaming crest, and remember other things—the things you see that you won't talk about, and the way you can wear out a whole tribe in your rutting?"

Nithrin gasped. It seemed to her that her blood congealed in her veins, her heartbeat and her breath suspended for an awful moment.

He knows, she thought. He knows it all.

"Get out!" she shouted when she was unfrozen. Anger boiled up in her and overflowed. "Get out of this house and this space and never come near it again!

"I swear by the teachers I mean it!" she screamed from the doorway at his retreating back. "I never want to see your hateful face again!"

2

On her bed, Nithrin lay curled in a tight ball.

Night came, and she did not move.

What have I done? she whispered. She was afraid to examine the consequences of her action, afraid to even think of going through her days without Marek. Her teeth chattered and she rolled herself more tightly.

No one else had ever meant anything to her. But now that he had spoken her secrets, had dragged them into the light and thrown them at her, his knowledge would always be between them. Could she ever look into his eyes again?

She clenched her fists until her fingers ached. Other males would bring her hides and meat and firewood, but who would tease her out of black moods, would make her laugh with his silly animal faces, would sit with her in the long winter darks when every sound made her shrink with the fear of shureks?

If only she could take back her words! She had acted blindly, without thought. If she had stopped to consider. . . .

She realized now that Marek had never repudiated her,

for all that he knew. He had, in fact, protected her from even the fact of his knowledge.

She could have won him back with tears and soft words. He would have forgiven the lost eggs—he had before. This time, though, she knew that she had truly driven him away, and she would never feel safe again.

She kept to her house all through the next day, though Cuma and Orkas called to her about ripe seedfruit and she heard singing from the trail. She couldn't allow anyone to see her. For distraction from her thoughts she took down every one of her ornaments and polished them, then worked on the soiled fur until it was restored.

It was all useless. She could find no pleasure in pearly shells and soft pelts while a phantom Marek continued to accuse her.

She went to bed early and unfed, and slept badly. In the morning, driven by hunger, she considered opening her winter stores, but better sense prevailed. She knew that she had to go out, or her seclusion would put the seal of truth to whatever talk might have begun.

Spears of sun penetrated the canopy, tiny bright splotches that danced on the carpet of needles. Summer scents hung trapped: saps and warm leaves and a whiff of sweetness that set her mouth to watering.

It was the smell of seedfruit, and it came from the trail. Nithrin followed it to where Marek waited, squatting beside a full basket. She moved to circle around him, unprepared for the meeting, but she couldn't force her feet to obey. The scent of the plump yellow spheres obliterated everything but the gnawing pain in her stomach.

She seized the basket and ate with no regard for daintiness, until her fingers and face were sticky with pulp. When she had spat out the last seed, she turned to Marek with a laugh that masked her shame. "How did you know I hadn't eaten for a day?"

He sat without moving and studied his feet. "I watched your house and saw that you didn't leave it." He ventured a narrow glance upward at her face. "You should be building up your strength, not fasting."

"I was afraid to go out."

"Afraid of me?"

"Yes. Of what you might say. To the others, about me."

He rose to his feet. "Do you think I would ever harm you?"

"I didn't know. What you said . . . that you know everything. . . ."

He held out his hand and she took it, the familiar rough, strong grasp. He was her own height, and lean with a wiry toughness that put her in mind of the dipu, bending with the worst storms but never breaking. "Of course I know about you," he said. "I always have. But do you think it makes a difference to me? If it did, would I be here now?"

She almost believed him. "But don't you worry about my being so . . . strange? It isn't in any of the patterns we were taught."

"You make too much of those patterns," he said. "We all do. Look, every one of us is different. Pellen is a good tree climber. Cuma tried to be when we named her, but she doesn't like high places. So she's a diver instead, and no one thinks less of her. I hunt and Boroni works stone and Mim makes pots and you find things. What difference does it make how you do it? You have no need to be so afraid.

"And as for the other—the rutting fever—it's just the same. Zarn has a huge appetite for meat, and Nols for klava. Both do themselves harm, but yours—it doesn't hurt anyone."

"Not even you?"

His grin was wry. "A little, yes, but it's an old hurt and I've made my peace with it." He squeezed her hand. "Let's not talk about that, though. Now or ever. Just know that I understand how it is with you."

They dropped hands and walked together properly, with no contact, but Nithrin still treasured the pressure of his fingers. They spoke of inconsequential matters, by mutual consent avoiding the subject that weighed heavily between them. Nithrin felt giddy with relief.

Beyond the shade of the dipu grove it was warm enough to shed outer furs. Marek tied both of theirs into a bundle and swung it from his back, and Nithrin basked in the rare pleasure of sun-warmed skin.

"Nithrin! Marek!" Pellen, perched cross-legged in the fork of a rintu tree, waved greetings with a long, sinewy arm. She added a respectful salute, and Nithrin beamed as she responded.

The trail crossed a runnel of clear water. They stopped to drink, and Nithrin washed off the stains of her breakfast. She remembered her greediness and regretted it. Now she would have to pick more for another meal. "Are there any seedfruit left?" she asked.

"No, we worked over the bushes well yesterday," Marek said. "Orkas took most of the big ones for the drying racks, but everyone had a good feed." He squinted up at the sun. "If this weather holds, there may even be a second ripening."

"I hope so, though now"—Nithrin patted her stomach— "I can't be too concerned. I don't know when I've eaten so well."

Relieved not to have to venture after all into seedfruit brambles, Nithrin agreed to accompany Marek while he cleared a trail to an old hunting blind that he wanted to try again. They followed established trails oceanward through thinning trees, toward a brackish marsh where longbills had nested in the days of Smallsun.

Zarn and Roko appeared from the cross trail and detained Marek with talk about hunting. Their manner toward Nithrin was as courteously admiring as ever. Zarn agreed to help Marek, and Nithrin walked between the two males as the trail narrowed.

Zarn was from the landing before Nithrin's, but he had lost toes to frostbite and walked with the gait of an old one. Marek set a slow pace, and Nithrin followed dreamily. The sun caressed her shoulders, and she knew that it struck flame from her crest. She walked with studied grace, as aware of Zarn's eyes behind her as she was of Marek's backward glances. She seemed to move in a bubble of contentment more precious to her for the danger she had escaped, so that when they were overtaken by Rowan and the fish girl she closed her eyes, willing the bubble to remain.

The two would have circled off-trail and Nithrin would not have had to look, but Marek stopped them. He spoke to Rowan: "That longbill you brought down the other day—was it flying toward the marsh?"

"That or the ocean." Rowan seemed to follow Marek's thoughts. "Rintu wondered, too, if they were returning to nest. But I haven't seen any others that were close. He says you used to have a blind. Are you going there now?"

"Yes. Would you like to come?"

Nithrin aimed a nudging kick at Marek's ankle. She continued to avert her eyes from the fish girl, who stood sheltered behind Rowan. What could Marek be thinking of? He knew her aversion to the deformed female, and Embri's two egg-issue went everywhere together.

Rowan, however, quickly rid her of her fears. "No, Issa and I are going to the birthpool to relieve Embri. Suri has taken her hatchling out, into her house, and Embri is alone there now."

Nithrin shot the young landling a furious glance. How dared he talk in her presence of such sickening aberrant behavior? Especially when he had that gross creature with him, the result of one such flouting of the patterns.

Rowan was tall and straight and even pleasant to look at, with eyes and a mouth that resembled Rintu's. But the fish girl ("Issa," he called her, though it was no true name; she had never been admitted to the tribe) was a monstrosity to warn anyone from such experimenting.

Nithrin felt compelled to look, for all her revulsion.

Though the fish girl moved into the trailside cover, Nithrin saw enough. The rest she remembered.

The creature was more stunted in size than Embri had ever been, though she was five cycles out of the water. She had a lumpy, scarred skin, a flat face with a lipless mouth and almost no nose. Her crest was a mere scaly ridge, and most horrible of all—Nithrin stared in fascinated horror— were her abbreviated arms that ended in finlike hands with a rubbery skin stretching between the fingers.

Nithrin made a choking sound and turned away. Rowan stepped off the trail, too, and placed an arm around the fish girl. He continued to address Marek as though Nithrin had merely nodded. "Let me know what you find. That long- bill's meat was the best I've ever tasted."

He caught Nithrin's eye and smiled directly at her. Marek said something more, but Nithrin did not hear. She was sud- denly light-headed, with the intense awareness that presaged one of her seeing-spells. She felt the fish girl's confusion and Rowan's defiance assaulting her in waves, and she knew that in minutes she would reveal her own deformity to all of them.

She covered her face and ran down the trail. Through her fingers brightness wavered and shimmered, and she stubbed a toe and stumbled.

She dove into a patch of green that resolved itself into a low-branched copse. Well hidden, she sat without moving until the spell passed.

It had been mercifully short. She heard Marek and Zarn calling, brushed herself off and returned to the trail. This time, she had an easy explanation.

Zarn found her first. "Are they gone?" Nithrin asked. She clasped her arms and shuddered.

Zarn patted her shoulder until he saw Marek approaching, then quickly removed his hand. "I understand how you feel. I don't know why Rowan brings her among the others—he knows that she is alive only on sufferance."

Marek joined them. "This *is* a back trail," he said. "They weren't exactly parading through the village." He regarded Nithrin with less sympathy than Zarn had shown her. "Rowan was distressed when you ran. We all were."

Nithrin allowed her head to droop. "The sight of her makes me ill."

"Nithrin isn't alone in that," Zarn said defensively.

"Yes, I know." Marek touched the skin of Nithrin's cheek, which was still clammy. The stern lines of his mouth eased. "Perhaps you should go back to the village."

Zarn scowled. "I think, if she rests a bit. . . ."

Nithrin smiled at them both. "No, I'll go on. At least as long as there's a good trail."

They fell into the same formation. Zarn huffed as he struggled to keep pace while shouting up to Marek. "I still think you should have made Embri give that fish girl back to the ocean. We all did when we finally saw her."

Marek walked faster. "Embri refused."

"Then you should have cast them both out of the village." Zarn labored for breath, but he persisted. "And why would you let her try again, with such a one in her house?"

Marek stopped and turned to face Zarn, his eyes on Nithrin as well. "If your memory were as sharp as it should be with your quickness to accuse, you would remember that we all made the fish girl what she is. Embri had to take her out of the new pool before it was time, or our females would have let the ocean in. She had to hide the hatchling, and without seawater it couldn't form properly.

"Look at Rowan, and you know that hatchlings can be raised. Can be and must be. Of course I've let her try again, and this time I've promised that no one will interfere."

Zarn looked quickly at Nithrin, and she indicated by a slight hand motion that he should say no more. "Yes, Rowan is as fine-looking a landling as any in the tribe," she said to Marek. "We females all think so."

Instead of being pleased, he only grunted. They continued in silence until the trail ended in an impassable thicket of white canes.

Marek and Zarn hacked their way through. Nithrin followed and threw aside the cut stalks until she raised a blister and Marek made her stop. Her encouragement was all the help they needed, both males insisted.

The ground underfoot turned marshy. Nithrin waited at a

dry spot while the two males searched for the frangi copse that had hidden the old hunting blind.

They returned streaked with mud and sweat. "The cane's grown too high," Marek complained. "And those frangis probably came down long ago."

"No sign of longbill nests, anyway," Zarn said. "At least, none that we could see."

Marek squatted beside Nithrin. "Do you think . . ." He spoke with obvious reluctance, studying his hands. "I was wondering if you could help us. You know, when you find things. Could you . . ."

Zarn gave an excited yelp. "Of course! If you could look through the cane and tell us if there are nests. If there aren't any, we can all go home. Those canes are murderous."

"Nithrin?" Marek tried to meet her eyes, but she refused to look at him. How could he do this to her? she thought. In front of Zarn, too, who was such a talker.

It was just possible that she could bring back the seeing, since she had had it so recently, but it was the last thing she wanted to do. What if she couldn't control it and went into the kind of bad spell where she lost consciousness? And with Zarn watching so avidly . . ."

She couldn't risk it. For the sake of her peace with Marek, though, she had to pretend. "I'll try," she said.

The two males made sounds of approval. Nithrin closed her eyes for a moment, then stood and surveyed the marsh.

"No good," she said. She tried again, with a great show of blinking and wrinkling her brow.

She turned back to her companions, shaking her head. "No, it won't work. The feeling isn't right. I'm sorry."

Marek stood, too, and squeezed her arm. "Thanks, anyway."

Zarn seconded him. "I think it's futile to spend any more time here," he said to Marek.

Marek agreed. "If we continue to see longbills, I may return later. Back in the days of Smallsun . . ."

Zarn snorted, and Marek did not continue. Nithrin, too, hated talk of that time. The other sun had vanished soon after she had landed, and she knew nothing of seagreens for the gathering, of oceanfests or summer long-days when it was never dark. With furs and stores and a warm house, her present life was good enough. There was nothing to be gained by harking back to a better time.

Bigsun vanished behind clouds as they retraced the trail, and Nithrin wrapped herself again in her furs. Zarn invited both her and Marek to share his evening meal. He had trapped a large digger, he said, and there was more than enough if he made a stew.

They both accepted. Nithrin was not fond of the rank-tasting meat, but she couldn't well refuse an offer of food.

Zarn used red tubers and new shoots of tallgrass to disguise the flavor. Afterward he brought out klava, and the three sat talking and laughing until well past dark.

Nithrin leaned on Marek as they made their way to her grove. The crisp night air quickly cleared her head, but she continued to welcome the support of his arm. They stood for a time outside her house, idly recounting the events of the day. She was reluctant to have it end, until Marek grew serious and destroyed the mood. "You could have brought on the sight, couldn't you, there in the marsh?" he asked.

His voice bore no rancor, but Nithrin became instantly wary. "Perhaps I could have tried harder. But with Zarn there. . . ."

"I know." He still spoke gently. "Someday, though, you must get over being afraid. If you could use your gift fully, for the benefit of the tribe. . . ."

"But I do."

"I don't mean just finding lost bracelets. If you could show us where there is game, especially in winter, and tubers. Which trees are rotten and which ground will sink. Things of importance."

"But I can't do that!"

His silence and the pressure of his hand told her that he knew better and that he understood her reluctance.

It was nothing she wanted to discuss, however. She

yawned, half deliberately. "I'll come to see you tomorrow," she promised.

Marek heaved a sigh. "If we lived in the same house, like Rintu and Embri, we wouldn't have to be parted."

In spite of the klava, Nithrin felt a chill. It was an old refrain, and one she had hoped not to hear again so soon.

Nothing had changed between her and Marek, she thought. Neither the good nor the bad. She gave him the sign of dismissal and entered the house quickly. Though she did not look back, she knew that he remained for some time staring at her closed door.

3

Marek dragged the thick branch into Nithrin's tree space. "I'll cut this up for you tomorrow," he said. "Then, I think, we can pile it against the low wall and have Rintu extend the roof to cover it. Like he did on his house. You've seen it, haven't you?"

"No, I never go there. But it sounds like a good idea." Nithrin smiled her approval. It was not too early to prepare for winter. It always came too soon, and last time her wood shelter had leaked.

Marek brushed bark from his arms and massaged a purple welt. "I don't mind doing this for you, Nithrin, you know that. But have you thought how the same wood could warm both of us? It would be so much easier if we . . ."

"Don't. I don't want to hear it." She turned her back and started for the house. If he was going to begin that again. . . .

His grip on her arm halted her. "Why won't you even discuss it?"

He pulled her down to sit beside him. She started to protest, but thought better of it. She might as well hear him out and get it over with.

Marek traced a twig through the ground needles. He drew a box that enclosed two circles. "It's worked for Embri and Rintu. And last winter Orkas and Nols shared a house."

"Because his collapsed and she felt sorry for him. He has his own now. Embri and Rintu—well, they've been raising those hatchlings. But us. . . . There is no reason at all for us to give up our own space."

"Except that I'm happiest when I'm with you, and you say that you feel the same. It's usually me, anyway, when you mate, so why can't we be a true pair like Embri and Rintu?"

She opened her mouth, but he forestalled her. "No, I'm not talking about raising hatchlings. I know how you feel, so forget about that. I only mean living in the same house. And don't tell me what the tribe will say. They'll accept it. After all, I am headman."

Nithrin sighed. How could she dissuade him without giving offense? In some ways, she admitted to herself, the idea had merit. Especially in the lonely winters, when she didn't see her neighbors for days. She tried to think how it would be to have Marek always with her. A strength and a warmth against the night.

But always to be there. How could she live without her inviolate space? She rubbed out Marek's drawing and traced her own: two wavy lines, close but not touching. "No," she said. "It isn't our way, and never will be. 'A house for everyone,' the old ones sang. You ask for too many changes."

"It's clear: you don't feel toward me as I do to you." His words were toneless. "Perhaps you're afraid of being unsatisfied, in those ruttings of yours? Is that it?"

She recognized both a hurt and a threat. Anger drove her to strike back. "And perhaps your true concern is to cage me. What's clear to me is that you lied when you said you had accepted me as I was. I'm beginning to think, too, that all of your concern about the eggs was also a pretense. That you didn't care as much about raising a hatchling for the tribe as you did about binding me to yourself."

Marek clasped his hands between his upthrust knees. He delayed answering while he examined the taut gray skin of his knuckles. "Perhaps you are right," he finally said. "Partly, at least. I do suffer when you go to others." He raised his eyes. "Embri and Rintu mate only with one another. We could do the same."

"I don't believe it's possible," Nithrin said. "We may want to, but when the heat comes, you know how it is. I don't see how Embri and Rintu do it. I've heard that about them, too, but I don't believe it can be true."

"Have you ever asked Embri how she manages?"

"You know I don't talk to her."

"Well, I talk to Rintu, and he's told me. When Embri feels the first signs of rutting, she sends a message to Rintu if he is not at home. She stays in her house until he comes, and admits no one else."

"What if he is off hunting? What if she can't wait?"

"She can and she does."

"I don't believe it. And what about Rintu? Has he learned to ignore the rutting smell of every other female?"

"He avoids them. I know that that is possible, because I have done it myself."

"Really?"

"Truth." He made the sign. "I haven't been with any other female for I can't remember how many cycles. I haven't wanted to."

She touched his hand. His confession, unnatural as it was, somehow pleased her.

"Couldn't we try it?" he begged. "If we lived together, the other—the constancy—wouldn't be so difficult. Either house—you choose which one."

She pictured Marek's ugly hunter's lodge, and then his knives and spears and shaggy pelts among her own treasures. She knew her answer, but she pretended to consider. "Perhaps, in the winter," she finally said. Why anger him now? Much could happen before the cold season came. He might even give up on the idea.

It proved a vain hope. Marek brought more wood and piled it, but he continued to pressure her. The warm days did not last, and there were no more longbills sighted and no second ripening of seedfruit. When the ocean fogs returned to obscure the sun, Nithrin felt winter breathing on her.

Her stores grew. Pellen traded nuts and gourds for a lim shell necklace. Cuma brought seagreens—a gift for the mussels. Using the sight to forage on her own, Nithrin dug enough tubers to trade for anything else she needed.

She was ready to face the cold season. Alone.

Rintu and Rowan reinforced all the houses, and Marek pressed harder for her to give in. When three old ones completed the change and drowned, his arguments became an intolerable harassment.

Marek was obsessed with the dwindling of the tribe. Only thirty landlings remained. He named them for Nithrin on his fingers when he returned from the rites for the last bloated body. "Two more," he amended, counting the newest hatchlings. "If it weren't for them. . . ."

Nithrin had heard the whispered talk. She knew that Suri's hatchling toddled on spindly legs and that Embri's, still in the pool, had begun to lose its waterskin. She had refused herself to go to look.

"Embri and Rintu sing to the hatchling every day, in turns," Marek said. "Embri even swims with it."

"Embri and Rintu are gathering stores for Suri. They are talking to Orkas, who is near her eggtime."

"Embri and Rintu. . . ."

Nithrin had to clamp her lips to keep from screaming. Was she to hear about those two forever?

Though Marek noted her distress, he did not ease off. "I know how you feel about them," he said. "You would change, though, if you talked to Embri. If you went to see them."

"Never. And if you continue to go on about it. . . ."

Her threat was as plain as the unspoken ones he held over

her. They were almost enemies, she thought. Yet neither could do without the other. If only they could go back to the time before Embri had broken their patterns and upset all of their lives.

Marek watched her closely for signs of rutting, and Nithrin knew that for all his promises it would be the same battle if she proved fertile: pleas to preserve the eggs, more threats and constant arguments.

She could have no peace as long as Embri and Rintu were there to be held up as examples. For her own preservation she had to discredit them, and as the time drew near for her heat to come, she knew how she had to do it.

Boroni agreed to help. They planned it together, he driven by old resentments and she by a force that was even stronger. She would live her life again on her own terms, and Marek would see that she had been right all along.

When she felt the first signals of her rutting, Nithrin wrapped herself well against any scent and went to tell the big stonecutter. He sped to do his part and she hastened home, the fire kindled in her before she reached her door.

She moaned as she paced the five steps back and forth. If only he would come . . . Soon, she would be driven to go out, and the plan would be ruined.

She heard Rintu's call and went to the door.

She signaled him to enter, first her space and then the house.

"What is it, Nithrin? Boroni said you had to see me right away, and . . ."

She opened her clothing. Rintu moved back, but not far enough. "Why are you doing this?"

Even as he spoke, she saw that he was caught. She watched him struggle against himself, almost making it to the door and then returning. She lowered herself to her bed, and he was on her. His cries and his thrusts were those of rage, but she rose to meet him eagerly. In minutes she was lost to all sense of time or place.

Dimly Nithrin was aware that Marek came to the door, that there were shouts and a shaking of the walls. A part of the chimney fell in, and when she lay at last calm in Rintu's arms they were both covered with dust.

Rintu got up with rude haste. "He is out there," he said. He dressed himself and looked about wildly, as if somewhere in the room he might find a means of escape.

"There is nothing I can do," Nithrin said. "You must face him."

At the doorway, Rintu turned. "Why?" he asked again.

"You know that you've always wanted me," Nithrin said. "Marek knows it, too."

She dressed slowly. Her loins still felt thick and heavy, and she knew that the heat would return. This time, though, she would have to endure it.

She heard nothing from outside. When she went at last to look, there was no one in the clearing.

She had expected a bloody fight. Surely Marek would not have gone docilely away, not after what he had done to the house.

The quiet became more and more ominous. Nithrin suffered through a second swelling of her sex, unappeased, afraid now for herself and cursing Marek for what he had made her do.

When her body was hers again, she set to work cleaning up the mess from the chimney. Anything to distract herself from her fears. She went outside to survey the damage to the walls, and there was still no one in sight.

Marek had probably ambushed Rintu in the forest, she thought. And the longer he delayed coming to her, the better.

Still, the dipu grove was in darkness before she heard running footsteps approaching the house. Her fears returned: why was he in such a hurry after delaying so long? And to enter her space without permission. . . . The visitor did not even stop at the door. He pulled open the doorflap and crouched, panting, in the opening.

It was not Marek at all, but Rowan. "I know it is your doing," he said between gasps.

Nithrin's first impulse was to order him out, but curiosity

overcame her outrage. She motioned for him to stay where he was, well away from her. "What has happened?" she asked.

"Just what you planned."

He came in anyway, and she edged back. "Truly, I don't know. Marek came upon me and Rintu when we were mating, and I've been crazy with worry all day about what he might do. Are they both all right?"

Rowan uttered a harsh bark of a laugh. "Save your false concern—neither is harmed. But Marek has exiled Rintu. Embri, too, as she insists on going with him."

Nithrin clasped tight fingers. "Can he enforce it?"

"The whole tribe will; they are outlawed for life."

She struggled to suppress a cry of triumph. It was better than she had hoped.

"Marek pretends that it's because Rintu attacked him—a lie—and because of him and Embri breaking so many of the patterns. He claims that the tribe can support it no longer. Everyone knows, though, the true reason. Rintu told me how you trapped him."

"And you believed him? You must be the only one in the tribe who does." Nithrin detected a flicker of doubt in Rowan's eyes, and pressed on. "I'm no friend to Embri, everyone knows that. But I'm sorry for what happened, and truly—I didn't plan it. Why should I? I have as much to lose as Rintu from Marek's anger."

"But Rintu said you sent for him."

"Of course I did. I was going to ask him to build onto my roof—over the wood. I didn't know I would be rutting when he came. I was just as dismayed as he was."

"Have you told this to Marek?"

"No, I haven't seen him since . . . he came upon us."

"You must talk to Marek. He's like a madman. He thinks Rintu knew, that he had been watching you."

Nithrin pretended surprise, then thoughtfulness. "Maybe it's true. He wouldn't be the first."

Rowan groaned. "How can you think that? You must be affected with madness, too." Nithrin shot him a glance of outrage and he appeared to recollect himself. He spread his hands in appeal. "You must go to Marek and explain. He will listen to you."

Nithrin held up her own hand. "No, I have nothing to say. And even if I did, he wouldn't listen. Marek hates me now. It's best for everyone if I stay away."

Rowan's face was bleak.

"When must they leave?" Nithrin asked.

"They're making ready now. They are to be gone by morning, by full light."

"The fish girl, too?"

Rowan scowled. "Her name is Issa. No, she will stay with me. The hatchling can't leave the water yet, and Issa will take care of it. She and I and Suri."

We'll see, Nithrin thought. Rowan rose to leave, and she watched him disappear into the blackness of the grove.

She stood by her door for some time. The forest had a strange feel to it—a restlessness. Torches flickered on the trail, and she thought she heard a far-off keening. If only she knew what was happening. Now, when she wished for the sight, it would not come.

At dawn, she took back trails to Embri and Rintu's house. Early as it was, she found most of the tribe already there. She had intended to watch from a distance, but Cuma spied her and pulled her into the crowd of spectators that milled about in front of the free-standing structure that was such an insult to all of them.

"Start your own tribe, you two!" someone shouted.

"Maybe the shureks will take you in!"

"A whole tribe under one roof!"

"A tribe of hatchlings, all shitting on the floor!"

Embri ducked out and placed a bundle on the pile outside of the door. A clump of dirt hit her on the cheek, and she hurried back inside.

Rintu came out, carrying a spear. "Throw it!" Boroni taunted. He brandished his own weapon, and so did Marek and Roko and Nols and Zarn.

Marek looked up at the sky. "It is time," he said. The five spears thumped warningly on the ground.

The crowd drew back, allowing a wide pathway.

Embri and Rintu walked bowed under the weight of their packs. They crossed their space without looking back, though Embri winced at the despairing howls that issued from within the house. When they had disappeared into the forest, Roan led the weeping fish girl out, across the clearing to his own hut.

Pellen began the assault on the deserted house. She kicked the front wall until the chinking began to fly. Others quickly joined her, and in minutes the oversized dwelling was a ruined heap of dirt and mud-straw and broken beams.

Marek waited impassively, leaning on his spear. He had not looked once at Nithrin. He appeared as cold and hard as searock, but she could sense the anger smoldering inside him.

Nithrin had not joined, either, in the destruction of the house. She felt weak and slightly ill. Lack of sleep, she thought, until she felt the warning light-headedness.

She backed away, into the bushy cover at the edge of the clearing. The light came quickly, blinding as before. This time, however, she did not try to blank it out. She bore with it, fighting her pain, until she could focus through it. She looked into the forest and saw Embri and Rintu as clearly as if they were standing before her.

Not so clear was the crowd of small figures that surrounded Embri. The tiny shapes glimmered and wavered and finally solidified into the forms of shiny-skinned, naked, walking hatchlings.

There were dozens of them, all emitting a keening sound like the one the fish girl had made. Embri turned and pointed toward Nithrin, and the ghastly host started toward her.

Nithrin looked about for help, to Pellen and Cuma and Orkas where they stood over the wreckage of the house, but they, too, were surrounded by the shining figures. All of them began to advance on Nithrin, their hands outstretched and their mouths gaping.

She looked to Marek; he had to help her.

Marek, however, lay torn and bloody on the ground, his eyes glazed in an unseeing stare.

Nithrin screamed and fell insensible.

4

Nithrin heard whispery sounds like the buzz of blueflits. She opened her eyes to see a circle of anxious faces peering down at her. Her head was cradled in Cuma's lap, and Pellen and Orkas and Mim were chafing her hands and feet. Nols and Roko squatted close, watching with avid curiosity.

"She's awake!" Mim dropped the hand and moved back.

The whispers stopped, and Nithrin sat up. "Marek... where is he?" She looked around for the wounded figure she had seen.

Pellen answered, "He's gone. Hunting, he said. But you: are you all right now? What made you faint like that?"

Nithrin ignored the questions, still haunted by her vision. "Are you sure he wasn't hurt?"

"Marek was fine," Cuma assured her. "Why do you ask?"

"I... I had an idea he wasn't well. The way he looked."

"Well, he *was* quiet," Cuma granted. "But you know, it wasn't easy, what he did. Those two had always been his friends. I think he wanted to be off by himself."

"Did he say anything about me?"

"He saw you lying on the ground, and told Pellen and me to go look after you."

"Is that all?"

"Yes. He didn't talk much, he was so anxious to be off. We thought at first he was going after Rintu and Embri, to make sure they didn't turn back, but he took a high trail—the one up to the seeping spring."

Into shurek country, Nithrin thought. Alone. "Didn't anyone try to stop him?"

"We all did," Roko said. "But it was no use. He acted strange. He cut us off and no one dared argue with him."

"Where is everyone else?" Nithrin asked.

"They've gone to the pool," Nols said. "Embri's birthpool, to let that hatchling out."

"We waited for you," Mim said. "If you're all right, let's go now. We can catch up with them if we hurry."

Cuma and Pellen tried to help her up, but Nithrin brushed off their solicitous hands. "I'm fine. It was nothing. A bad stomach, that's all." She stood, and in a moment she did feel normal. The fear for Marek would not go away, but there was nothing she could do.

They went in a group, all except Orkas, who remained by the ruined house. "Aren't you coming?" Pellen called.

Orkas took a few steps, then stopped. Her egg-swelling distended the lacings of her outer fur. "I . . . don't think so," she said. She kicked at a broken pole. "I don't understand why you want to harm the hatchling."

"Embri again," Pellen muttered. She dismissed Orkas with a disgusted wave and turned to Nithrin. "She'll get over those ideas now. Marek should have gotten rid of those troublemakers long ago."

Nithrin said nothing. For all the success of her scheme, she could not dispel her unease. When they caught up with the others at the edge of the forest, she would have turned back if she could have done so without causing comment.

They all crossed the dunes north of the landing beach, then picked their way on island bridges across a stretch of sedgy marsh. Before them, on the sandflats that had been part of the old seagreen bed, the new pool glistened within a low circling wall of black rock.

Suri met them with a hunting spear.

"Be reasonable," Roko said. "You can't stop all of us."

She raised it easily, tall and strong as she was. "No, but the first one to take a step nearer will get this in the belly."

The males cursed their lack of weapons. Boroni growled behind Roko: "I can take her."

Before anyone could move, however, a shout from behind froze them.

"Turn back, all of you!" Two figures, also armed, emerged from behind a dune. Rowan and the fish girl. As they advanced, Rowan hefted his spear and the female swung a bola. Even with her stubby arms and misshapen hands, she whipped it in wicked circles.

"Her aim is deadly, make no mistake," Rowan warned.

With angry mutters, the group turned back. Rowan and the fish girl watched from a raised hillock. They lowered their weapons, but remained on guard.

"We'll only come again," Boroni said as he passed the two. "And next time, we'll be prepared."

Rowan ignored the threat. "Does Marek know what you're doing?" he asked. "He promised safety for us and the hatchlings."

"Marek!" Boroni snorted in disgust and moved on.

"Marek is still headman," Rowan called after him. "All of you: what will he say about this?"

Suri joined Rowan and the fish girl on the hillock. Nithrin looked back at them, her eyes drawn to the hatchling that clung to Suri's legs. The other one—Embri's—was a dark shape that swam in the pool.

Suri's hatchling looked exactly like the ones in her vision, even to the shine of its well-oiled skin. Its face and arms were normally developed, she saw; it would be no fish girl.

"I know—it doesn't look bad at all," Cuma said. She shrugged. "I'm glad we didn't kill the one in the pool. What would be the purpose?"

"We weren't going to kill it," Mim said. "Only free it to swim in the ocean as it should."

"Oh, stop pretending," Cuma said crossly. "You know what that would mean."

"Look here, Cuma..." Mim stopped and looked about for support. Finding none, she trudged on in aggrieved silence.

Nithrin, too, was relieved about the hatchling, though it wasn't her main concern. If she could only put her mind at rest about Marek....

She signaled to Roko and walked with him out of earshot of the rest. "How long did Marek say he'd be gone?"

"He didn't," Roko answered. "But alone as he is, I'm sure he'll be back before dark. We've seen shurek sign up that way."

"Would you go look for him?"

"For *Marek*?!!!"

"I know it sounds foolish, but I have a reason." She forced the words out of a tight throat. "I had a...vision. That's what was wrong with me before. When I fainted." She swallowed and plunged ahead, talking fast before she could change her mind. "I get them, you know. Like when I find things. Only this one was different. Clearer and—well—somehow stronger. I saw Marek hurt. Badly. Maybe it hasn't happened yet, but I know it will."

Roko gaped at her. "I...I don't know," he finally stuttered.

Suddenly, Nithrin didn't care what he thought. Only that he believe her.

"I've seen other things, many times," she said. "I saw where you buried that bag of killerfish teeth. The ones Zarn needed for his snare."

He gasped and stepped away from her, almost slipping into the marsh. "It was a joke," he said. "I was going to surprise him with it later."

"I'm sure you were." She gave him her full smile. "Now, about Marek. Will you go after him for me?"

Still he hesitated. "Why don't you ask Boroni or Damin? They're both better at tracking than I am."

"Boroni wouldn't go—you know why. And Damin wouldn't, either. He'd be too afraid. Afraid of Marek and afraid of shureks. No, you're the only one brave enough. The only one I'd care to ask."

They came to the dunes and turned aside, away from the route of the others. They squatted in a windless hollow. "I didn't know you thought so much of me," Roko said. His lips wore a half smile that quickly disappeared. "I can't deceive you, though. Even if I agreed to go into shurek country, I could never find him."

"I could," Nithrin said. "I'll go with you."

They left at high sun. Roko carried his hunting spear, and Nithrin, who had no skill with weapons, a knife that dangled awkwardly from her belt. They left their outer furs at the spring hut and traveled in body and leg wraps for ease and speed.

On the trail, Roko continued to worry aloud. "If Marek is all right, he'll be furious. He made it plain that he wanted to be alone."

"I'll take the blame," Nithrin said. "Gladly. But believe me, that's not what we'll find." As they advanced into the dense green stillness of the inner forest, she was more and more certain of what awaited them. Her senses seemed to sharpen and expand until the scent of blood and the pain of Marek's wounds were as real to her as her own breathing.

The blazed trail ended. There was at once a difference, a subtle change that had nothing to do with the vegetation. There were the same trees—gourds and dipus and frangis— and where they thinned, the same choking underbrush. But Nithrin knew by a prickling of her flesh that this was no longer their forest.

Roko stopped. "I don't know where to go from here."

Nithrin concentrated. "That way, along that ravine." Roko hesitated, and she plunged ahead. When he found evidence that they were indeed on the right track—a bit of stiff-cured legging on a thorny branch—he caught up with her and took the lead again.

"I'm convinced," he said. "You point the way, but let me go first.

"And quietly." He showed her something else he had found—a matted clump of hair the color of the greenish scum that formed on forest sumps.

Nithrin grew surer as they proceeded across the ravine and up a wooded slope where the air was thick with the fetid odor of shureks.

Roko appeared unaware of the smell, though he continued to advance with caution. Nithrin was strung tight as the web of a snare. The sight would be on her soon, she knew. She willed it to come quickly.

They came upon the shurek first, crumpled beneath an outsized dipu. It was dead, the blood already congealed around the protruding spear.

Marek lay a tree length away, in the brush where he had apparently crawled for cover. Roko turned him over, and the wounded headman groaned. His wraps were torn and dark with blood from the terrible claw wounds that covered his arms and chest.

Nithrin crouched by the two males and tried to see through a blinding haze. This time, she vowed, she would not succumb to it.

"Have to . . . get out of here," Marek mumbled.

"Nithrin, you've got to help me." Roko strained to lift the still weight of the headman.

Nithrin's vision still swam, but she rose. Shureks were territorial, and they were vengeful. She knew that there was little time.

No time. The dead creature's mate announced its presence with a bone-chilling yowl. Roko dropped Marek and seized his spear, but the enraged animal was on him before he could aim.

Erect, the four-footed shureks were half again as tall as a landling. This one dwarfed Roko as it towered over him, disposing of his spear with one swipe of a clawed foreleg.

Roaring, it raked with the other, a slash that opened Roko's shoulder to the bone.

Nithrin picked up the fallen spear. Time held itself suspended as she looked into the creature, at the pumping sac that sent out its blood. The spear was too heavy for her to throw, but she knew exactly where to aim as she leaped with it.

Her force sent the shurek toppling, the spear buried in its heart.

Roko was up to finish it off, but he declared it already dead. "I don't know how you did that, but . . ." He swayed, and Nithrin helped him to sit. Blood welled from his shoulder.

Nithrin was faint herself as her vision returned to normal. She had never learned healing, or wanted to. Nevertheless, she somehow bound up both wounded males with strips from her wraps.

Roko was pale as death, but fear seemed to give him back his strength. He and Nithrin together got Marek to his feet, and half dragging the delirious headman, they stumbled down the slope.

Brambles tore at Nithrin's skin as they crossed the ravine. Marek's arm was clamped tightly over her shoulder and he was conscious enough to take stumbling steps, but his weight sent shooting cramps into her neck and back. She had to steel herself to keep from crying out. Roko, though wounded, bore his share of the burden without complaint, and she could do no less.

When Marek collapsed again they were back on their own trail, not far from the spring. Nithrin felt safe enough there to remain with Marek while Roko went for help.

Marek jerked convulsively, and Nithrin turned cold with panic. She lifted the makeshift bandages. The wounds were dry, but inflamed with the poison of the shurek's claws. It would be better for him to bleed, she thought. She tried to open the wounds by pressing them, but Marek moaned so piteously that she gave it up.

"Live!" she held her mouth to his ear and pleaded. "You must live, for me and for the tribe."

Boroni and Nols came with a pole-bed. "Suri is taking care of Roko," Boroni said. "She is mixing something to draw out the poison." He shook his head at the sight of the headman's pale face. "He looks far gone. Roko will probably be all right, but this one. . . ."

"Can't you hurry?" Nithrin urged. They settled Marek on the litter and set off as fast as they could manage over the uneven ground. Nithrin ran beside them, her eyes on Marek's staring ones. They were beginning to glaze, and a froth issued from a corner of his mouth.

Suri inspected Marek and looked up with a grim face. "I'll need help. Nols, get Orkas over here as fast as you can."

Nithrin stepped forward. "I can do what is necessary."

"You?"

"Yes, we must not lose time."

Suri gave her a curt nod. "Wash him, then, with this." She handed Nithrin moss and a bowl of bitter-smelling brown liquid. "If he bleeds, good." She motioned to Nols and Boroni to hold Marek, and Nithrin laved the wounds while the headman thrashed.

Suri brought another bowl, of something thick and steaming. "Here, help me with this," she directed. Together they spread the paste on gourd leaves and tied them to Marek's chest.

When he was poulticed, Marek lay quieter. "Is he better?" Nithrin asked.

"No, it is a bad sign when they are still," Suri said. Marek breathed with a harsh rasping sound.

"What else can you do?"

Suri's hands moved deftly among her hanging array of herbs. "He must not be allowed to sleep." She pinched and crushed, and mixed the results with klava.

Boroni held Marek up while Nithrin and Suri tried to get

him to drink. He swallowed once and choked, then swallowed again.

"That is enough," Suri said.

Marek blinked and looked around. "How did I . . ."

Suri wiped his face. "Roko and Nithrin brought you out of the forest."

"Roko . . . I must . . ." He coughed up blood, but would not be stilled. "Send for Roko. And bring me the cape."

"No!" Nithrin cried. "You will be well!"

"Do as he asks," Suri said to the males. She turned to Nithrin. "Keep him calm. There is nothing more we can do."

Suri retreated to a corner of the hut where her hatchling was rousing itself from sleep. Nithrin knelt over Marek, letting her tears fall on his face. "I am so sorry, for everything," she sobbed. "I could never be . . . what you wanted. I could never give you what you wanted."

He opened his hand, and she put hers in it. "It was enough." He closed his eyes, and he was gone.

5

Three cycles later, toward the end of winter, Nithrin waited in her house for the headman's visit. She rehearsed in her mind what she would say to him.

Orkas needed food for her brood—the male youngling Targ, now nearly fully grown, and the two summer hatchlings that ate like ravening tuskers. Rowan and the fish girl had depleted their stores to help, as had Suri. Nithrin herself had given what she could, and urged others, but the winter had been long and everyone was feeling the threat of hunger.

Roko did his best as headman, Nithrin granted, but he was no Marek. There would never be another like Marek, she thought with an ache that time had not dulled.

Marek would have known how to persuade the villagers to part with some of their stores. He wouldn't have had to cajole or threaten; merely to explain with his quiet reasonableness the necessity of such sharing for the survival of the tribe.

The survival of the tribe. It had been his mission, and now it was hers. Her atonement. Marek would live through her, she had decided that last time she had held his hand. Now it seemed that sometimes he did. She had known his thoughts so well that it was easy to imagine what he would say and how he would act to solve every village problem.

Roko thought that Marek somehow communicated with her, and she encouraged the belief. He was so in awe of her that everyone in the tribe knew he was headman in name only.

Nithrin heard Roko's call, but she did not go to the door. She should have been there, ready with a wave and a greeting. It was his due as headman, but it amused her to keep him waiting like any other visitor. She slipped a last bracelet on her arm and moved without haste to admit him.

Roko stood at the edge of the clearing, and she motioned him in. He looked toward the house, but she denied him that. They would meet in the open, where anyone passing by could see them and wonder at their weighty talk.

Patchy snow covered the ground under the dipus, and there was no place to sit. Nithrin indicated that they should walk, and they headed up-trail.

"I can't ask anyone to starve themselves because of Orkas," Roko complained. "It was her decision to raise those hatchlings."

"I think she expected Nols to help her, especially with the last two. He doesn't mind bragging about them, I notice."

"I still think it's unnatural, knowing what you've spawned. Suri at least doesn't put that label on anyone."

"Suri's different. She has a good trade and could raise a hatchling every year without difficulty. But Orkas. . . ."

He grimaced. "I know. She had trouble even providing for herself. But what can I do?"

"*Tell* everyone to give; don't ask. And no one will starve. Tell them I promise that."

"You've seen it?"

She nodded. She hadn't, but Roko didn't know. He believed whatever she told him, and only half the time it was true.

Her real moments of sight still came on her unpredictably.

She no longer tried to hide them, and scorned those whom she made uneasy. Her body was as smoothly supple as ever and her crest stood up without a blemish, and for all her strangeness she had no shortage of eager partners when she rutted.

"Orkas's spawn are handsome and healthy," Nithrin said. "We can't afford to lose them now." Except for the malformed one of Embri's, she thought, they had all turned out well, the new breed of land hatchlings. Eight now. Embri's three, with the youngest male, Dak, mostly raised by Issa; Suri's two females, Linnit and Chula; and Orkas's three—Targ and the small females, still unnamed.

Marek had been right to encourage the births, Nithrin acknowledged now from the security of her high standing. She was safe. No one would expect her to take on the burden herself, but the tribe was still dwindling and other females had to be persuaded.

Marek could have done it, or Embri and Rintu. But now it was up to her.

She adopted Marek's tone, a trick she had mastered. "This summer, we must take more care when we distribute stores. Hatchlings that cannot forage must receive a share from everyone."

"There will be complaints."

"Not so many if more females have hatchlings by the end of summer. You must speak to Cuma and Pellen again. And to Mim."

Though it was frost-cold, Roko wiped sweat from his face. "You know, it isn't . . . fitting . . . for me to do that. Before, when I spoke to her, Pellen ordered me out. Me, the headman!

"And it does no good." His face mottled darkly, and he plucked at the skin of his neck ridges. "They say what can I know of such things? They say I have no right to even speak of it to them. I am shamed, and it accomplishes nothing."

Nithrin considered. "Perhaps you are right." Roko was her instrument, and to have him undermined would do her no good. "Let that go for now." She smiled at his immediate sigh of relief. "The best persuasion is a well-formed hatchling, and Orkas's will provide that in double measure if we continue to get them food."

"I'll see to it."

His promise put an end to that problem. They moved on to the next, a naming ceremony for Dak and Linnit and Targ, of a size now to join the tribe. "We'll hold it as soon as the snow melts," Nithrin said. "Boroni and Rowan can make a trip down the coast for seagreens, and if they find any, perhaps we can even manage a small feast."

"Rowan insists that we include the fish girl in the ceremony," Roko said. "He wants her to have a true name, 'Issa.'"

"No!" Nithrin glared her indignation. How could he even mention it? She had never overcome her aversion to the web-fingered creature. Only the memory of Marek's wishes had kept her publicly tolerant, but nothing could ever persuade her that the fish girl was a true landling. "It isn't to be considered," she said flatly.

Roko offered no argument. Nithrin had nothing else to discuss, and she dismissed him.

She smiled at the alacrity with which he scampered away. She knew how he hated these meetings, hated the power she held over him. The one time they had coupled, he had been so unnerved that even in full scent it had ended disastrously.

She never mentioned it, of course. Even Roko could be driven too far by humiliation.

She took a down-sloping trail to the meadow by the pond. The land was still blanketed with snow, but if she could bring on the sight to see what lay beneath. . . . Once she had located a nest of soft-shelled scudders, and another time a pair of ergips in winter sleep.

She held herself motionless, suspending even her breath, and stared at the white until her eyes ached.

Nothing came, however. The pain was wholly physical, not the inner one she sought.

Disappointment flooded her. She had tried repeatedly, but she had never yet learned to control her visions. Sometimes she had been near, but when it seemed she was on the verge of seeing, a veil would fall and she would remain on the other side.

This time, she had not even come close. She stamped her numb feet and turned from the field. She would have to wait for the spells to come in their own time, and act quickly when she felt the first warnings. If she had luck, by the time of the naming feast she might be able to provide something to supplement seagreens.

They all needed the release of a celebration, she thought. But there had to be food. It was her omnipresent concern, for the tribe now as much as for herself. Winter stores would be depleted, even the tallgrass seeds that Dak and Linnit had collected, that cooked so surprisingly into a sustaining mash.

She studied the snowpack. Another four hands of days until melt, she estimated. She should find something in that time.

A spell came on her when she was visiting Cuma. She ran outside immediately and searched the entire clearing with her inner sight, but she discovered only a single clump of withered tubers. Still, Cuma dug it up and was grateful.

Nithrin had also seen what was growing in Cuma's belly. "Have you thought, this time, about raising a hatchling?" she asked.

"You know? But of course—you always do." Cuma lifted the tubers from her wash pan and shook them dry. She carried them inside, and Nithrin followed. "Yes, I have thought about it." She put the tubers aside, laid sticks on her low fire and blew up a flame.

Both females squatted and warmed their hands. "I never thought I would change my mind," Cuma continued, "but I see those two smallest ones of Orkas's often now that they can walk. Run, I should say. They chase each other all through the grove." She smiled. "I like to see them."

"Then why don't you have one of your own?" Nithrin settled herself more comfortably. "Roko will see that it gets a full share for winter stores."

Cuma's smile broadened, then subsided. "I don't know. In some ways . . . I just can't decide." She looked hesitantly at Nithrin. "How about you? Would you ever consider it?"

The floor was suddenly hard, and Nithrin shifted. The fire was too hot.

Cuma continued. "Others would, too, if you did it. We've talked."

Nithrin wiped her face. "But why should it depend on me?"

Cuma stared hard at Nithrin's anklets and her bracelets and the collar rings between each neck ridge. She touched the silky fur of Nithrin's cloak.

Nithrin's skin prickled. She felt her crest stiffen, and hot words waited on her tongue.

Cuma, however, couched her reply in inoffensive terms. "Because of what you are. You know: the red flower. We all think, if it's all right for you. . . ."

Nithrin rose; she no longer felt like visiting. "Save the tubers for the namefeast," she said.

Cuma followed her out, the question still in her eyes.

Nithrin ignored it, and Cuma did not press. They parted at the trail, to Nithrin's relief. She hurried home, so disturbed that even the sight of green shoots poking through the melting snow of the meadow did not cheer her.

She closed her doorflap and sat in the near darkness. She seemed to hear Marek's voice in the old litany: The tribe. Her duty. She spread her fingers over the swelling on her belly and mouthed a silent speech of protest.

She, too, had seen Orkas's matching egg-issue many times. They were so wild that Orkas tied them to a leash when she went out with them. Her house, Nithrin had heard, was a shambles.

Suri's Chula was quieter, and it was said that she could already name most of the healing herbs. But Nithrin remembered the last rainy summer when both Suri and Orkas had lived at the pool, when Linnit had been sick and Suri had traded all of her furs.

Nithrin closed her eyes against tears, clasped her arms

and rocked herself. Gradually the comforts of her soft floors and the knowledge of the wealth on her walls worked their soothing magic. Marek reached too far, she decided. And Cuma was impertinent.

She had given the tribe her sight, and that was enough. Pellen's grove had water and Boroni had his hardstone, and the hunters knew better which trails to take. If she could, she would even provide a feast, the first in uncounted cycles. Yes, she thought, she had satisfied her debt.

The snow patches shrank to slushy puddles. Nithrin had a lucky vision and located a tree cuma's cache of nuts and dried sourgraks. Damin and Nols brought in a single-horn grauf, and the feast became a certainty. When Roko reported that the team had left to search for seagreens, he and Nithrin set a day for the naming.

The team had only been gone a day when Rowan appeared at Nithrin's clearing. She heard his call and invited him inside the house where she was cracking nuts on her hearth. "What happened?" she asked. "Is Boroni all right? You must have found a new bed of seagreens to get back so quickly."

Rowan folded his long legs as he lowered himself to the floor. "I didn't go," he said.

"But . . . didn't Roko send you?"

"I had other things to do." He held up his hand. "Dak went instead. The trip will be good training for him."

"This is what you came to tell me?" She pounded her stone on a stubborn shell. How like Rowan, to deliberately flout her. She hid her displeasure, however. If he came to provoke her, he would be disappointed.

"No, I came to ask you about Issa. If you had changed your mind about giving her the mark."

She smashed the shell with a vicious blow. "Roko is the one you should talk to about that."

"No, I know it's your decision." He picked up the fractured rintu and picked out the meat. He handed it to her with a look that was as beseeching as his proud bearing would allow. "I don't know why, but it's important to her to be accepted by the tribe." He touched his shoulder over the mark. "If I could, I'd give her mine. It means little to me."

Nithrin forgot her resolve to be aloof. "How can you say that! The tribe . . ."

"Yes, the tribe." His mouth twisted. "I know how much it means to you. To everyone. But will the tribe bring back Embri and Rintu? Will it make Issa beautiful, or even make her look like other landlings? What has the tribe ever given but pain to those close to me?"

"Dak will be named. And Issa"—Nithrin forced herself to say the name—"she has been allowed to stay in the village."

"As an outcast! Does anyone ever talk to her? Do you? Do you ever know that she has a beautiful voice and that she can sing all the songs of the tribe? Do you know how she longs to be like others?

"Do you know, Nithrin, that she admires you more than anyone, that if you once spoke kindly to her, she would consider it the greatest happiness she has ever known?"

Nithrin became very busy with the nutmeats, arranging them in a bowl. She motioned to Rowan that he should leave.

He ignored the command. "You pretend to be doing Marek's will. I know—Roko has told me. What about Issa, then? Marek would have taken her in."

"I don't know that!" His rudeness was insufferable, and even worse was having to justify herself to him. "Marek wanted the tribe to be strong. How can it be if we take in someone like her? What useful service could she perform?"

"She has already done more than most. Dak would not be alive if she had not cared for him after Embri left. And last summer, with Chula and with Orkas's pair of egg-issue—if you had ever gone by the pool you would have seen her there every day. She knows more than anyone in the tribe about raising hatchlings."

Nithrin stopped her work. She placed the bowl carefully on the hearth. The idea that was forming in her mind needed more thought than she could give it now, but if it were possible. . . . "Would she . . . raise one not her own?" She fought to keep her voice steady. "I mean entirely, if the female did not wish to burden herself with it."

"I think she would be honored. Issa can never be fertile. She is . . . malformed . . . that way, too. But yes, as well as I know her, I feel sure she would take another's." He looked at her boldly. "Especially if the hatchling were yours."

"I didn't say that!" She turned away to hide her agitation. "You must leave now."

"What will I tell Issa?"

"You will tell her nothing. I promise nothing. Do you understand?"

She scarcely heard his reply or saw him go, her mind was so unstrung. She emptied the bowl, then filled it again with the same nutmeats. She picked up her pounding stone and put it back down.

Voices clamored in her mind. Marek's, from long ago: *You must be the example.* Cuma's: *Others would, if you did it.* Rowan's: *I think she would be honored.*

She would have given in, for all her personal aversion, except for something else that warred with the familiar voices. It was a directive without words or even sound, but nevertheless compelling. The echo of a watersong from another life.

It had been her answer when she had hungered to know the light world above the ocean and the old ones had fed that hunger with their song pictures of an ordered landlife and a final return. Those pictures had included no molting hatchlings in enclosed pools. There had been no scab-skinned little terrors who cried for hours and destroyed houses. Only

> *Sunlight falling soft through sheltering trees,*
> *A safe house, a private house,*
> *Laughing days with friends, and quiet nights.*

Nithrin seldom thought of the waterlife; at least not consciously. Yet she had always tried to live according to the pattern of the songs, even knowing that with the loss of

Smallsun the patterns no longer fit. What she was contemplating now, what the landling voices told her to do, would be a betrayal.

Torn, she refused to think at all. Only klava shut out the voices, and it took a full bowl before the watersongs were extinguished as well.

6

Nithrin dressed with studied care for the namefeast. She wrapped her winter thinness in a length of soft-cured grauf-hide that almost duplicated the shade of her well-oiled skin. For a mantle she selected a chulafur with spots of darker gray, all of it a foil for the vivid hues of her crest.

There would be sun, she saw with satisfaction when she stepped outside. She touched the scales of her crown and smiled; it would appear at its best.

It would be a fine feast. Boroni and Dak had brought backpacks bulging with new and tender seagreens. Damin was preparing the meats, the smell of fire and cooking wafting into the grove. Nithrin's nuts and sourgraks filled a heavy pouch; more than enough for everyone.

She had made no decision about the issues that disturbed her rest. Her egg-swelling was barely visible, so that matter was not urgent. The other—Rowan's request—she had put in abeyance, too. She had hoped for a vision to point the way, but none had come. She trusted to her instincts to guide her when it came to the actual ceremony.

It was not yet high sun, but Nithrin found the meadow already filling with early arrivals. The ground was damp, but not soggy. Tiny blue and yellow flowers dotted the green, and someone thrust a garland into her hands.

She smiled her thanks and settled it around her shoulders. Damin greeted her and led her to the fire. Spits of meat and pots of stew suspended on frames sizzled and simmered over glowing embers. Other pots sat on hot stones near the fire. "What do you think? Will there be enough?" Damin was naked except for a loin wrap. A grin split his broad face. His skin glistened with sweat and grease.

Nithrin inched back from the heat. "It looks perfect. Everything does. You've done well, Damin."

He laughed aloud and shouted, "Yi-ee! This will be a feast to remember!"

Another scream, a high-pitched imitation of a skyhunter, rent the air as Nols zoomed running by the fire and seized a chunk of finger-burning meat. He screamed louder and Damin pursued him, shouting epithets.

The klava jars, Nithrin saw, had already been opened. She looked around for Roko; he should have guarded them until after the ceremony.

Roko came from around the fire with two branding stones. "Boroni carved a new one. What do you think?"

She inspected the raised cross-in-the-circle, feeling the well-defined edges. "Yes, it is better. Use it."

Roko tied the selected stone to a treated hardwood pole and placed it to heat. He turned to Nithrin. "Will you lead the chants? Everyone will expect it."

Nithrin felt a rush of pleasure, until better sense tempered it. It wasn't her due, and she wanted no bad feelings. "Mortha is the oldest. And there are many before me. Pellen, Mim, Suri."

"Mortha has started the change, and she doesn't want to show herself. I've spoken to the others, and they agree that you should be the one."

"Then, yes." The pleasure returned. She checked the figures in the clearing, counting. "As soon as everyone is assembled, I'll call them to the circle."

Roko arranged the folds of his white cape. "Rowan came to see me again."

"I know. He visited me, too." She searched the clearing for the tall form and the misshapen short one; they would be together.

The fish girl, though, was alone. She responded to Nithrin's gaze with a ducking motion of her head and started hesitantly toward her.

Nithrin waved Roko away. She moved from the fire to a clear spot in the meadow. Issa came closer, and Nithrin waited. When she recalled what Rowan had told her about the creature's admiration, she straightened her bearing to appear more regal.

The fish girl wore a cape that covered her arms and hands. She could not disguise her dwarfishness, however, or the grotesque contours of her face. She halted at a respectful distance and looked down at her hide-wrapped feet. "Rowan said I should . . . come to speak to you myself, but I was afraid. I thought you wouldn't want to see me." Her voice was throaty, but not unpleasant.

"So you want a name?"

"Yes, a true one." She looked up with a roll of her protruding eyes. She clasped her hands under her cape and gasped.

The sun was behind Nithrin, and though she was well aware of the effect it produced on her crest, she was taken aback by Issa's reaction. The fish girl stared at her with an open mouth and an expression of undisguised adoration. It was homage beyond any Nithrin had ever received, or even dreamed of, and for a long moment she basked in it.

Then she became uneasy. "What is it? Why are you looking at me like that?"

"The colors," Issa whispered. "The shining." Then she sang in a soft, low voice:

Out of the flames
The red flower
Sun struck
All glory.

Nithrin stood bemused. "What is that song? I've never heard it."

"I made it. It is yours now—if you like it. . . ." Issa continued to gaze at Nithrin, offering her soul in her eyes.

Roko interrupted them. "Everyone is here but Rowan, and Dak says not to wait for him."

Nithrin recalled herself. "We will begin then." She nodded to Issa. "Join the others."

"You mean. . . ."

"I mean Dak and Linnit and Targ. They know what to do. They'll tell you."

She heard Issa's yelp, and then she put everything else from her mind. The call required concentration. She had only heard it twice, at her own naming and at Rowan's, and she had never practiced it.

She thought back to that first ceremony, when everything had been so new to her and yet so familiar. Drawing on those memories, and on ones that went deeper than experience, she filled her lungs and allowed the ululation to well from her throat.

A single circle formed around the four initiates. Roko entered it with the glowing stone. Targ flinched as the brand seared his shoulder. Linnit closed her eyes at her turn, but neither cried out. Dak took his mark with complete stoicism, as did Issa, whose only distress appeared to be at having to remove her cloak.

Since the new tribe members already had their names, Roko needed only to confirm them. He repeated the names and the callings they had chosen while Nithrin led the chant.

"Landling—tribe member—trailmaker—Dak.

"Landling—tribe member—hunter—Targ."

Linnit received the title of potter, and when she came to

Issa, Nithrin paused for only a second. "Singer," she said firmly.

Surprise rippled through the circle. Nithrin went directly into the chant-before-feasting, and the official part of the ceremony was finished.

Nithrin sat between Cuma and Pellen as the bowls and jars went around. In spite of her resolution to eat daintily, her face was soon as smeared with grease as anyone's. She groaned and patted her stomach. "Why did I do it?"

For an answer, Pellen belched mightily. Cuma giggled and couldn't stop, and finally had to run for the bushes.

Roko produced a jar of klava that had been aging for three winters. He signaled for the name-dance, promising the treat to the three who remained longest on their feet.

Orkas's pair of younglings raced in and out of the line of dancers. Pellen tripped and Mim collided with Damin, who cursed roundly and tried to catch the miscreants. They escaped, to wreak havoc on the leftover food.

Orkas sat in a klava stupor. Just as Nithrin was about to scream at her to see to her younglings, the fish girl took charge of them. She caught them both, slapped and scolded them and led them away.

Soon Nithrin heard laughter and splashing from the direction of the pond. Suri disappeared there with Chula and returned alone. Nithrin congratulated herself: she had acted wisely concerning Issa, who would be a singer for the land-raised hatchlings as the old ones had been for those in the sea. She smiled to herself and relaxed completely, the first time she had been able to do so in days.

The dances and contests continued. Boroni bested everyone in wrestling and spear throwing, and Mim won the foot-race. Dak and Linnit and Targ, all of them puffed with importance, engaged in thick-tongued conversation with the headman.

Cuma was the first to see the four figures as they came out of the forest. She clutched Nithrin's arm. "Who can they be? I thought everyone was here."

The sun was in Nithrin's eyes, and she could only tell

that the approaching shapes were those of grown landlings. Then she recognized one—Rowan, of course. And the others. . . .

"It's Embri and Rintu!" Cuma exclaimed, jumping to her feet. The fourth was a stooped, long-nosed male with a lame leg. A landling whom Nithrin had never seen before.

Cuma and Pellen joined the press around the newcomers. Nithrin remained seated, all her pleasure in the day replaced by confusion and a mounting dread. She heard the exclamations and the questions as if through a blanket of moss, not even curious enough about the stranger to listen. Only one matter concerned her: her guilt and how she could protect herself.

The two exiles had looked thin but otherwise fit. They had walked in boldly, as if, knowing of Marek's death, they considered their sentence revoked.

Nithrin relived that whole damning episode. Embri had never liked her, and now she would surely expose her. She recalled Rintu's anguish: *Why are you doing this? Why?* Embri would not have needed to ask, but at the time she, like Rintu, had been powerless.

"Nithrin!" Boroni squatted before her, his face mottled. "You must do something. Everyone is welcoming them back as if they had only been out gathering muscales. And Roko is gaping like a fool. They were *exiled*!"

"I know, but that was in Marek's time."

"Then let me get Roko. You must tell him what to do."

"No, don't call him. And stay away from me." Nithrin covered her face with her hands. She wanted only to escape notice.

Boroni shook his head, bewildered.

"I tell you, I don't *know* what to do," Nithrin said. She sat rigidly still until Boroni left. Her mind raced, but it gave her no answers. She considered sneaking away. If she could hide in her house until it was all over. . . .

But no, it would never be over. Embri and Rintu were sure to stay, and her absence would be an admission that she had something to hide. Perhaps if she pretended a vision, to remind everyone of her power. . . .

She would do it, she decided, if the confrontation went against her.

"Come and hear what they're saying." It was Cuma, urging her to join the crowd. Nithrin rose and followed her, but remained well back.

"Yes, another tribe," Rintu was saying. "Like us in many ways, though the speech is different."

"Can you talk to him?" someone asked. It was Dak.

"And who is this?" Embri asked.

Rowan laughed. "Don't you know your own hatchling?"

"No, he was still in the water when I left." There was a silence. Nithrin inched forward to see Embri inspecting Dak. "What do they call you?"

"Dak. The trailmaker. See." He displayed the new, raw mark.

"I'm glad you have that name," Embri said. "It is a good one. The other Dak, the last one, was brave."

"They say that I am, too," Dak said. "I've been on a hunt, and I went with Boroni for the greens."

Embri looked as though she would take him in her arms, but Dak drew back. Embri smiled faintly and turned to Rowan. "You and Issa raised him well." She searched the faces around her. "I don't see Issa. Where is she?"

"At the pond, with the new younglings," Suri said. "I'll get her."

Embri continued to admire Dak, and Rintu answered more questions. Yes, he could talk to the stranger, whose name was Broken Tree. It had been Tall Tree before his accident. Their names were all like that, he said. It was their custom to always use two words: Bright Shell. Fast Water.

Murmurs of astonishment gave way to more questions. Rintu held up his hand. "I will tell it all, but it is a long story. Shall we sit and be comfortable?" He led the way back to the fire.

Again Nithrin stayed in the rear. Roko joined her. "What do you think?" he said. "I can't even remember why we were so against them before. There's no reason, is there, why they shouldn't stay?"

It was clear to her what answer he expected. She shrugged. "I suppose not." She certainly didn't want to be a focus of Embri's anger. Both Embri and Rintu looked so strong and confident. And they appeared to have the tribe's support.

Everyone settled again in a circle, with Rintu in the center. Embri and Broken Tree sat behind him, flanked by Rowan and Dak. Nithrin sheltered behind Cuma, on the opposite side, making herself as small as possible.

Before Rintu could begin, Suri came back with Issa and the three younglings. Embri left her place to run to meet Issa. They embraced tearfully.

Embri led Issa to the circle. "You've grown taller. Yes, I'm sure you have," Nithrin heard her say as they passed. Issa pulled aside her cloak to show Embri the brand. She turned and pointed to Nithrin. "She did it. She took me in. It's not true, what you said and what Rowan said." Her flat face was suffused with happiness.

Embri looked at Nithrin for the first time. She took a step forward. The stubby scales of her crest stood up stiffly and she expelled her breath with a hissing sound.

Nithrin froze. *Now it's coming*, she thought.

Issa plucked at Embri's mantle. "Please, listen to me. You're wrong about her. She's as kind as she is beautiful."

Embri looked from Nithrin to Issa. She studied the fish girl's face with a puzzled expression. Finally, she sighed and relaxed her stance. "It's your day," she said.

Nithrin breathed again. Issa and Embri and Suri and the younglings all found places, and Rintu began to talk.

Part III

RINTU'S TALE

When we left the village, Embri and I, we had no idea where to go. I thought we should hide out in the woods not too far away, in the hope that Marek would cool down in a couple of days and we could come back. But Embri pointed out that that wasn't likely, not considering who—or what—was behind it all.

Embri had lived by herself in the forest before, you remember, and she wasn't as frightened of being alone in it as I was. Not that she wasn't heartsore about our being cast out—she had left a hatchling behind, as well as Issa who still needed her. And she was plenty angry, too. Enough to have taken a knife to the face of a certain female if I hadn't stopped her.

But afraid? Not her. Embri knew we could survive, and the truth was she'd always wanted to see what kind of country lay beyond our bit of beach and forest.

We had been north before, when Rowan was hatched, and neither of us liked the looks of that coast. We knew the way was easy south, at least as far as the seagreen cove, so we decided to go there first and supply ourselves.

We had stores with us, of course, and warm furs and hunting gear—snares, bolas, knives and a long and a short-spear apiece. If anything, our packs were too heavy, but we couldn't decide what to part with. So for two days we struggled under those big loads, camping on the beach, until we came to the seagreen beds.

Many of you have been there, though I don't know if anyone has ever gone into the woods inland. We did, and it isn't so different from here. The trees are mostly dipus and frangis, with some gourds that didn't seem to be bearing any better than ours. Embri found signs of small animals—diggers and ergips and cumas—and of some larger ones, luckily none of them dangerous. We found no shurek traces at all.

I wanted to stay, to build a house far enough into the forest that no seagreen gatherers from the village would ever know we were there. We could see Rowan, if he came, and any others who were friends, and not be entirely cut off.

I even started the house—a stone-walled one I had been thinking of for some time—carrying rocks from the beach. Embri, though, wasn't satisfied. She said that as long as she'd had to leave her home and give up her hatchling, she wanted to do a lot more exploring.

I tried to talk her out of it. It was getting cold by then, especially at night, and I thought we should settle in for the winter. We argued for several days, and finally we each gave in a little. I put a makeshift roof on the house and we cached most of our supplies. Our plan was to explore up into the second range of mountains that you can see from the beach, coming back as soon as there was a threat of frost or snow.

We couldn't go south, which was our first choice. We tried it, and had to turn back. The beach ends a day's journey below the cove, in a barrier of black, jagged rock that you can't cross or go around. We followed it inland a ways looking for a break, but we couldn't find one. In places it's so wide you can't see across, and it goes on I don't know how far into the mountains.

Anyway, Embri wanted to see what the high country was like. I'd heard the old story about the spirits who live in fire pools up there. You remember the one, Boroni—Krull used to tell it. About the water spirits and the fire spirits, and how they fought over the world until they finally divided it between them. Krull and Lors both said that none of us could ever live beyond the dividing line, which was the first mountains, but when I told Embri about it she only hooted. "Has anyone ever tried it?" she asked, and I had to admit that they hadn't, as far as I knew.

That settled it for her; she had to be the first. You all know how stubborn she can be, and me—well, I certainly had no reason anymore to worry about what the tribe would think.

No, if ever two landlings were free, it was us. I'll admit I wasn't as eager as Embri, but I figured we'd turn back before we ever got to those second mountains.

I was wrong. We had light packs, and it was easy going at first. Game trails and not much underbrush. We found plenty of water, and usually we had a dry place to sleep. With the seagreens, we were all right for food. We'd taken a few snares, and Embri knew where to set them at night so we usually had some kind of meat in the morning.

Our biggest danger was of getting lost—you know how the woods can get you turned around. We took the sun for our guide, as well as one cone-shaped peak that lay ahead. Embri measured our shadows twice a day so we'd stay on a course, and we tried to keep it straight—over windfall trees and down gullies and over outcroppings of rock. There wasn't anything to see but more forest, and ahead, those purple ridges that cut into the sky. Before I realized it we were climbing again, well into the high country.

Maybe there is something to that old story. Whenever I thought about how far we were from the ocean, I got a trapped sort of feeling. It was as if the forest and the mountains were pressing in on me and I would smother if I didn't get out. Sometimes it was so bad I couldn't breathe, and Embri would have to give me air from her mouth like she did for the hatchlings.

I know it was all in my mind, that there wasn't anything really wrong with me. It didn't bother Embri at all, but then she doesn't have all the do's and don't's in her that the rest of us got stuck into our heads when we were swimmers. All of us but Rowan and Issa, that is—and those three here you just named.

Lucky for them, I say. But we'll talk about that later. Anyway, there I was in the middle of this strange forest, all choked up and thinking every breath was going to be my last. Embri was as worried about me as I was sick, and we almost went back. But Embri talked in that way she has, explaining about the song patterns and how I didn't have to give in to them, and I calmed down and got better. We were pretty high up by then. Embri said if she could just see what was on the other side of the peak we were on, she would be satisfied. There wasn't any frost yet, at least not in the woods, so we went on.

The summit, though, was a lot farther away than it looked. I still got those choking attacks sometimes, but I learned how to talk myself out of them and we didn't lose any more time. We climbed so many days that I can't count them for you. All I can say is that we had worn out two pairs of footwraps apiece before the slope began to level.

Then the country around us changed. It was barren, with only a few trees here and there. They were different, too. The dipus were small and scraggly, and there were other trees that I hadn't seen before. They grew in clumps, with a loose white bark that twisted in folds around the trunk, and thin branches with long curling needles. Between these clumps of trees the ground was hard and rocky, and the only cover was a prickly bush with hard green berries. It wasn't more than knee high, but it was tough and made a ruin of our leggings.

There wasn't any game up there, at least not that we could find, and we were out of the seagreens by then. Embri was afraid to try the strange berries, so we were living on the dried rations we had brought. Our stomachs were hurting a lot and we were tired all the time, but we kept on going, more out of stubbornness, I think, than anything else.

We didn't see any fire pools, though by then it was so cold that I wouldn't have minded finding one. There may be some at the very top—I can't say, since we didn't go all the way up. There was another rise that we knew we couldn't make, so we circled around it until we had a good view of what lay beyond.

It was a sight that left even Embri speechless.

Below the belt of trees on the lower slopes was a stretch of something open that went on in waves like the ocean, to a dim line of more mountains almost too far away to see. No, it wasn't water, though there was a wide stream that snaked through it. Tallgrass, it must have been, mostly brown but still yellow and ripe in places.

I've never imagined there could be such a meadow. Embri was sure there would still be seeds to gather to make mash. She wanted to go down, even to winter there, but I held out for the stone house and our stores. What would we build with, I asked, and what kind of food would we find if there were no tallgrass seeds?

Embri pointed out the dots that were moving through the yellow and brown like some kind of grazing animal. When I saw that, I was tempted, too. For a while. But then I thought of the long stretch of mountains and forest between us and the sea, and I got choked up again.

I knew I couldn't live there. At least, not easily. And there was another thing: what would we do if Embri got fertile so far from the ocean?

She thought about it, and agreed that we should go back. We hadn't even made it to the other side of the mountain when it started to snow.

We fought a storm all the way down. Nothing around us looked familiar, but of course we couldn't expect to follow our exact trail. As I said, we'd been taking our directions from the sun, but now we couldn't see it at all, much less measure shadows. Also, I guess we didn't think about how the sun would move. We didn't know it then, but we were way off course.

When we got into the lower woods again the snow turned to sleety rain, and we headed to where we thought the ocean was. It poured without a break, and even under the trees we were cold-soaked. We hardly stopped to sleep or to chew a mouthful of moldy graks, we were so anxious to get back to dry furs and a hot meal.

You can imagine how we felt when we broke through the trees and were on the beach again, only nothing looked familiar. It wasn't the same beach we'd started from or even traveled down when we came from our village.

This was a straight stretch of black pebbly sand, covered with boulders and beaten by fierce winds, with no dunes or sheltered coves, and certainly no seagreen beds. When we hiked up north a ways we knew where we were: there was that spreading formation of black rock, cutting us off from our house and our furs and all of our winter food.

We tried to cross it, battling the wind, but we had to go on all fours and in minutes our hands were bleeding and our footwraps were in shreds. We gave it up and headed back to the near woods, to the shelter of a few spindly dipus.

Neither of us could think what to do. We couldn't get across the rock, and as for circling around it, for all we knew it extended all the way back to the mountains. Winter was on us, and we had to settle in somewhere. Embri thought of the grassy valley on the other side of the mountains and I thought of the snug stone house we should have been sitting in, and each of us blamed the other for being where we were.

When we were speaking again, we decided that we could drag ourselves a bit farther south, maybe finding a less exposed stretch of coast. We built a smoky fire under the trees and dried our furs as best we could, and we each sacrificed a piece for new footwraps. The storm let up some, and we set out again. We didn't want to take the time to hunt, and the night snares didn't catch anything, so we lived on stringy roots and even those wormy tree grubs that I never thought I could eat.

In a few days we came to another rise of mountains, this time one that ended in cliffs at the ocean. It wasn't a place where we would have chosen to stop at any other time, but with the snow coming down by then even by the water, we didn't dare go any farther.

We holed up in a sod burrow that we dug out and roofed in a day. It was in the lee of a slope, so we had some protection from the weather, but it was so cramped that you couldn't believe two people could actually live in it.

You do what you have to. I remember when Embri and I first shared a house, everyone asked me, "How can you give up your private space?" I'll admit it was hard for me at first, but that winter, in that hole in the ground, I would have laughed at them.

If I'd had any stomach for laughter, that is. We didn't think of anything but keeping warm and finding enough food to stay alive, and believe me I wasn't particular anymore about what it was.

Somehow, we made it. When the snow melted we hadn't much flesh left on our bones, but we both wanted to move on. Embri was near her eggtime, and we had to find a sheltered beach where we could make a pool.

We started south again. The mountains weren't high, and on the other side we found the first signs of Broken Tree's tribe.

2

We had been climbing, keeping close to the water, when we came to a spot where we could look down.

The short strip of curving beach below us was shut in by cliffs, and on the ocean side by a barrier of rocks that made an enclosed pool of the shallow water. We could see clearly to the sandy bottom, and there was no mistaking the familiar dark shapes that swam there.

Embri shouted and grabbed my arm. I hardly had time to get my thoughts together when I noticed something else—curls of smoke drifting up from the nearby woods. I remembered the old rumors about another tribe, and I don't know if I was more relieved that we weren't alone anymore, or afraid of what we might find.

Embri, though, could only think of that huge enclosed birthpool, and she was sure we would find landlings who were like us. She would have rushed right down, but I convinced her that we should be cautious. We circled around and came down from the mountain well behind where we thought their village must be, made a fireless camp and spied them out.

At first it didn't seem a proper village at all. The houses were all together in one clearing, with no trees or tree spaces between them. They were low and round, like giant digger mounds, and all different sizes. The landlings who came out of the houses, though, looked like Broken Tree here and like us.

We watched them for a day. It was rainy and mostly they stayed inside, but those who came out seemed to be searching for forest food much as we do. Several of them went toward the beach.

Late in the morning, about two hands of half-grown younglings crawled out of their largest house and ran into the woods. The crippled male who followed them was Broken Tree.

The little ones scattered all over the forest, which didn't have well-marked trails like ours. Suri, you wouldn't have believed it: no one was looking after those younglings at all. Broken Tree dug a few roots and then sat on a log and dozed. If he was in charge, he didn't seem to care at all about where they might be. A couple of them almost found Embri and me where we were hiding in a tree they tried to climb, but they kept falling off and finally gave it up. We listened to them talk to one another, but we couldn't understand a word they said.

At low sun Broken Tree made a loud whistling noise through his fingers, and the younglings straggled back to him. Most of them had found some kind of sprouts or tree-worts that looked edible, and those that hadn't, he punished with a kick or a cuff.

Embri and I circled to the village clearing again, but after dark everyone stayed inside their houses. We decided to show ourselves in the morning.

At first sun we surprised a young female who was checking a snare near our camp. She screamed and ran to the village, and by the time we got there everyone was out.

They are a big tribe, we saw—at least twice our number. There was some spear waving and a lot of shouting at first, but they calmed down once they realized we were no danger to them. I can't say that I blame them for being suspicious. We must have looked like wild creatures—starved as we were and dressed in filthy, ragged furs. And of course our words didn't make any sense to them.

We tried to show them by signs where we had come from, and one old male who was into the change made a long speech that seemed to satisfy everyone that we were harmless.

We were invited into one of the houses by a big male who wore a lot of ornaments. Their headman, we found out later. As many as could fit crowded in after us until we were jammed shoulder-to-shoulder. We all squatted—you had to, the roof was so low—and everyone kept shouting questions at us, louder and louder, even though they knew we couldn't understand. After a while we all shared a bowl of some kind of cold stew that had a suspicious smell and a worse taste. Embri and I both ate some, to be polite, but hungry as I was, I had a hard time getting it down. I didn't know then that it was fish, and it's lucky I didn't or I would have insulted the Sonsis by being sick on their floor.

That's what they call themselves—the Sonsi. It's from their word for ocean, and means "out of the ocean." They're not a bad tribe, though their customs are not ours. We came upon a lot of things like their fish-eating that disgusted us, but we learned some useful things from them, too. Their way of building houses, for instance, and the cloth they make out of bark and some new kinds of foods that we *could* eat. And of course, the way they raise hatchlings.

What's that, Roko? Yes, I'm going to tell you about the houses. You, too, Suri—I'm coming to that. All of you, sit easy if you want me to go on.

That's better. The houses first. They pile chunks of wood —so long and about this thick—in layers, one on top of another, and chink them together with clay until it's smooth inside and out. Before the roof goes on they burn a big fire inside the walls to bake the clay, and believe me those houses are warm and they don't leak. The Sonsis say they make them round so the wind blows right off them, but I don't know if I believe that. We could make them the same way, but in any shape we wanted.

Besides being warm, their houses are light inside, at least in the summer. Before the baking they take out one of the chunks of wood, so in the warm season there is a hole that lets in the sun. When it gets cold again they put back the piece and chink it up.

Yes, I thought it was clever, and I intend to try it. With stone, though—it should work just as well.

But back to my story. Embri and I stayed at first in the big house with Broken Tree and the younglings. We supposed then it was because it was the only one that had enough room, but later we found out it was because we were so ugly and tongue-stupid that no one else wanted us to live with them. We would have liked to build our own house, but when we tried to make them understand what we wanted, they just walked away from us. We were afraid of giving offense, so we went where they told us, and it turned out to be a good thing. We learned Sonsi words fast, from the younglings, and as soon as we could understand Broken Tree, he told us everything we wanted to know about his tribe.

They were losing numbers, too, he said, even though they had hatchlings in the enclosed bay. He himself had helped to build up the rock barrier, back when Smallsun had first started to fade. The Sonsi old ones had a watersong about Smallsun's going and coming back, he said, and everyone knew it. They also knew that until it returned, the hatchlings had to be penned and tended.

Embri thinks that our tribe must have had such a watersong once, too, but that it got lost. No matter: we found it again even without the old ones, and our way is better, we think, than that of the Sonsis.

We didn't say so to Broken Tree, but their ideas of "tending" are nothing like ours. Even with all the females in the tribe using the birth bay, they raise few younglings to full size.

Most are lost soon after they hatch. A keeper brings greens to the bay, but no one stands guard. And no one seems to care when the hatchlings die or are taken by sky-hunters or are swept out to sea when a storm stirs the waves over the barrier.

I suppose it's because the hatchlings belong to no one special. A female passes her eggs and leaves, and as far as she is concerned that's the end of it. The hatchlings that survive in the bay lose their waterskins early, like ours do, and then they go into another keeper's care, a female named Soft Sand, who tends them until they are able to walk. The ones in the house with Embri and me were from the last two summers. Broken Tree saw that they were fed and told them a few tribal stories at night, but during the day they ran free. If any of them came to harm—and two met death in the forest while we were there—no one shed tears or even made a deathsong.

Embri wasn't happy about leaving her eggs to such a risky fate, but she had no choice. As long as we stayed with the Sonsis, it was clear that they expected us to follow their ways. Neither of us wanted to wander anymore. Broken Tree had told us that shureks roamed the mountains and it was pure luck that we hadn't come across any. We didn't want to test that luck again, and neither did we want to spend another cold and hungry winter. So Embri went to the bay like all the other females, and we don't know if any of the eggs bore hatchlings, or if they lived, or even which younglings they might be if they survived.

At least they had a chance, which is something all of us should think about.

But more of that later. Let me finish now, and then we can all talk.

Embri and I stayed with the Sonsi for two full cycles. They treated us well enough—for ones they considered so backward and slow of speech—but we could never feel easy in their village. Imagine: no sheltering trees, and houses where one or two or three hands of landlings lived all together, males and females, in groups that changed with ruttings and quarrels and the need for a sewer or a hunter or—I never got used to it—a fish-catcher. I know, you might wonder that we minded such strangeness since we had been breakers of patterns in our own village. But again I ask you to imagine: talk, always talk, and the stink, for they never washed and they threw their leavings outside their doors; and worst of all, wherever you went, someone watching you.

Embri and I continued to live in the youngling house when it became plain that we would never be allowed our own. We replaced Broken Tree as keeper, a position no one wanted. It wasn't as bad as it could have been, but we began to think of the forest again, shureks or not. We thought of the seagreen cove where I had started a house, and we knew that somehow we had to get back to it.

Broken Tree had told us that it was impossible. The Sonsi had tried to go north by sea in the hollowed-out logs they use when they go out after fish, but the currents had always forced them back. He said that no one had ever crossed the black rock. Still, we were determined to go, even if meant climbing into the mountains again.

Surprisingly, Broken Tree asked to go with us when we told him about our plans. He would trust us to protect him from shureks, he said. He was tired of being the least in the tribe, and if we left he would have to be a keeper again.

We knew that he was stronger than he looked, in spite of his bad leg, and we agreed. Broken Tree said that no one would mind our leaving, and he was right. No one, that is, but the new keeper.

There was still snow on the ground when we set out. We wanted a full warm season to travel, though as it happened we didn't need it. Broken Tree, with a stout stick for support, slowed us down less than we had expected. We climbed over the first mountains in good time, and when we came to the rock barrier we found it to be partly covered with snow. We struck off toward the higher elevations, where it was still winter-cold, and found a spot where the rock was no longer jaggedly impassable. It was flat and white, covered with a thick sheet of ice.

We crossed it easily and found the seagreen cove. The stone house was still there, with the cached supplies undisturbed. The food was all spoiled, but it was no great loss to us—the seagreen bed was thick with fresh sprouts. Broken Tree and Embri brought down a grauf, and we all three wrapped ourselves in warm unpatched furs and feasted.

We were camped just off the beach, and barely had time to douse our fire and hide when we spotted two figures approaching. It was Boroni and Dak, though of course Embri and I didn't know then that Dak was our youngling. I still don't understand why Boroni didn't see our smoke, but you can ask him. As for the seagreens, we had gathered them carefully and the tide had come in, so the beds looked undisturbed.

The newcomers didn't seem to notice anything unusual. I crept as close as I dared and listened to them talk. Roko was now headman, I learned.

It was all I needed to know.

We were behind Boroni and Dak all the way back. We camped just below the village, and I waited to show myself until Rowan came our way alone. He said it would be a great surprise if we stayed hidden until the feast, and so here we are.

I've brought some of that Sonsi food I mentioned—these white seeds in the pods. Try some—here—you'll like the taste.

And now my throat is dry as dust and I'm ready for a good swallow of klava. Pass it over here; it's been a long time.

Part IV

THE NEW BREED

1

Ten cycles later, on a blustery day in late winter, a hatchling cried in the headman's house. Rowan put aside the notched stick with which he had been making a grain tally and rose to tend it. The tiny creature slept in a basket suspended from the roof by braids of hide, and sometimes a gentle swing sufficed to calm it.

This time, however, it did not. When the cries became strangled gasps, Rowan lifted the convulsed form from its wet moss and blew whispers of breath into the scaly slit of a mouth.

When the hatchling was breathing once more on its own, he replaced it in the hanging bed and rocked it until it appeared to sleep. Thick black waterskin still encased large portions of the hatchling's undeveloped body, and the new skin, where it showed, was raw and oozing. As he studied the pitiful creature, Rowan feared that his ministrations were futile. Nithrin had warned him when he and Linnit had taken it, half frozen, out of the pool. She had looked through the waterskin and seen that the new airsacs were not ready. "It is much too soon," she had said, "and even if it lives, it will be like Issa."

But what could they do? Leave it to die in the ice-rimmed pool? Linnit would have done so. She had already cried for it and sang its deathsong. Now she pretended that it was not in the cradle, and Rowan watched over it alone.

For five days he had not left it. The white cape, hanging prominently on the high wall, mocked him as he settled again to his housebound tasks. He should be out visiting other houses, distributing the last of the stored grain where it was most needed, instead of uselessly counting and recounting what would never last if the summer continued to be delayed.

He felt a surge of anger toward Linnit, but it did not last. He understood her apparent heartlessness: she had been disappointed too many times to risk it again. An entire clutch of eggs lost to a storm, fingerling hatchlings that mysteriously died, one stunted youngling that had lived a single summer —she would allow herself no more false hopes.

She had found escape from this latest grief in her clay, discovering somewhere a vein that could be worked. Rowan heard her in the front clearing now, experimenting with the new firebox that she had designed and he had helped her build. He walked to the door and watched her.

Linnit was tall and large-boned and dusky, like her eggsource Suri, with a bristly crest that was almost black. Her fingers were long and nimble, and even as a youngling she had loved to shape clay. Rowan had watched her grow up and had won her first rutting after a savage battle with his egg-kin Dak.

Embri had been furious with both males when she heard. "The next time, why don't you ask Linnit which one she prefers?" she had asked. They had done so, and Linnet had chosen Rowan.

He had been surprised. He was not headman then, and Dak had been Linnit's playmate. Rowan had not at first intended a permanent arrangement, but he and Linnit had stayed together for five cycles now, content—or so he thought—except for their inability to raise a hatchling. The repeated losses were harder for her than for him, Rowan knew; he supposed he should feel grateful that she had her absorbing work.

Linnit squatted in the mud at the stone oven. She was wearing only a single body wrap, but she seemed unconscious of the ocean wind that penetrated their winter-bare grove. She saw him and waved. "It worked . . . I think," she called. Her small, bright eyes gleamed as she held up a reddish-brown bowl.

Rowan checked the hatchling, which was still sleeping. It would be all right for a few minutes, he thought. He wrapped himself in a cloak and picked up another one for Linnit.

The red bowl was perfect. Rowan held it carefully, admiring it, while Linnit removed the other pieces. Her pleased expression turned to dismay as she examined one after another and discarded them. "Cracked . . . broken . . . cracked," she muttered. She threw a handful of shards across the clearing. "Two good ones out of all that!" She jumped to her feet and kicked angrily at the jumble of ruined pottery. "Maybe Mim was right, and the open fires are better. And I thought it was such a clever idea!"

"I still think it is," Rowan said. He turned the bowl in his hands, feeling the smooth surface and thumping it. "I can tell this is harder than any you've baked the old way." He picked up the other intact piece, a wide-mouthed water jar. "Wait and see: this one will never leak."

Linnit's scowl faded. "Maybe not." She studied the jar, and showed a hint of a smile. "Even Mim will have to admit it looks a lot nicer than the old black ones. And I won't have to show her these." She nudged one of the broken pots with her foot.

"I can use them to make roofs and chimneys," Rowan said. "Your work isn't wasted. And next time, you'll do even better."

Linnit squatted again and peered into the oven. Her bony legs stuck out at sharp angles and her cloak fell off. Rowan rescued it from a slushy puddle. "I'll take these two pots into the house," he said.

Linnit nodded, but did not look up.

Inside, all was quiet. Too quiet. The cradle hung motionless, and Rowan knew without looking what he would find.

Gently he removed the dead hatchling and wrapped it in the moss. He took down the ropes and the basket, placing them in the corner where Linnit kept her extra utensils.

She seemed not to see him leave with his small bundle. Once more he felt the bitter resentment that she could so wall herself off, and this time it did not go away.

He left the body at the water's edge after he had sent out his own song of grief. The wind blew in sharp gusts, and the thick fog that had blanketed the beach when he arrived had lifted and rolled back, to lie in long vapor veils over the water. Below it the ocean stretched immense and gray and threatening. He felt no affinity for it, no sense at all of the beginnings that Rintu spoke of so often. Gazing out at the surface of the world he had never known, Rowan wondered as he often did at the difference between the younger landlings like himself and those like his egg-sire who had had waterlives. Even Embri admitted that the old way was the natural one for their kind, but Rowan could not make himself believe it. How could it be true when he and the other land-raised hatchlings, with no water memories to hold them back, had done so much to make all of their lives easier? The older tribesmen could never have invented Targ's short-spear shooter, Nimo's digging blade, Chula's tally sticks or his own baked clay building blocks. Or most recently, Linnit's firebox. All new things and all useful.

But then there was the cold bundle at his feet. According to Rintu, it would have been frolicking in a gentle, watery world.

Rowan wiped his wet cheek. Perhaps there was something to be said for the old patterns. However, they existed now only in the minds of a few. In time they would be entirely lost. The reality of this ocean was an icy pool and a dead hatchling. It was Rintu and the punishing return he would soon be making.

Thinking of such endings, Rowan decided to pay his sire a long-overdue visit. He had been putting it off, always uneasy with anyone in the change, though Rintu, to give him due credit, was taking it better than most.

Better than Rowan could comprehend. To spend his last hours in there. . . . Rowan looked out again at the expanse of white-tipped waves and shuddered.

Black specks of skyhunters appeared in the distance, and he left the beach hurriedly. In the dunes he saw Issa, coming from the direction of the common birthpool. Probably overseeing the morning feeding, he guessed; she took her responsibilities seriously. He stopped to allow her to catch up.

"The hatchling died," he said.

Issa reached up to touch his arm. "I thought so. I saw you on the beach."

Rowan frowned against her show of sympathy. His was not the only loss. "How does it look at the big pool?" he asked.

"Not good. Most of the new hatchlings are eating, and don't seem to mind the cold. The bigger ones, though— they'll never make it if this weather doesn't change soon. I thought of taking a couple of them out."

"Don't do it. You can never keep them alive."

Issa nodded. "I know. I talked to Nithrin yesterday, and she said the same thing. I hated to leave them, though. One of them has skin that is starting to crack, and it looks so miserable. I wonder whose it is."

"It's just as well not to know." Rowan felt his mask of composure crumbling. He turned his face from Issa to stare at the ground. "I wish now that Linnit and I hadn't made our own pool," he said. "The other way, we could always imagine that one of the new crop of younglings was ours. I don't know if I ever want to go through this again."

"You don't mean that!" Issa exclaimed. "You can't! You and Linnit have just had bad luck. Next time you'll have a healthy one."

"No." Rowan continued to gaze down at his feet as he struggled to express thoughts that had troubled him for some time. "I don't think it's possible. I've wondered . . . in fact, I'm sure . . . that it's a weakness in me. Like you, Issa, only on me it doesn't show. You know that Embri was just learning to raise hatchlings, with both of us. Any mistake she would have made . . ."

"What are you saying? That you can't have young of your own? But Linnit's eggs have hatched many times. You just left one that did back there on the beach."

"Yes, and neither it nor any of the others were fit. You've seen it over and over—it's only the strongest that live." He looked up, past the dunes toward the birthpool. "No, it will never be one of mine in there."

"That isn't true! You mustn't think it, not for a minute. Believe me, I know." Issa's head jerked like that of a sandhopper with the vehemence of her denial.

Rowan was taken aback. Such loyalty, he thought. Flattering, but a shame for it to be so sadly misapplied. He shook his head in reproval. "Little one, you may be the best hatchling tender in two tribes, but there are some things even you can't know about."

She bridled, waving her truncated arms. "Don't act the headman with me. I know what I'm saying—that you *can* have your own hatchling." She pointed a webbed finger. "That you already do, in fact."

"What are you talking about?"

"About the second one I raised for Nithrin. Arak. He's yours, you know."

Rowan was stricken dumb.

It couldn't be. But then again, it just might. . . . Memories whirled, and conjectures. "That's the . . . it's the craziest thing I've ever heard," he finally stammered. "Why, I don't think Nithrin even knows who . . ."

"She does, and she's told me. So you and Linnit mustn't give up hope. It can happen again."

Through Rowan's confusion, one worry surfaced. "You won't tell Linnit?"

"Of course not! I wouldn't even have said anything to you—I promised Nithrin—but you were talking so foolishly."

He relaxed somewhat, though he was still bewildered. "Arak." He sounded the name aloud, picturing the male youngling who would receive his mark in the summer ceremony. Tall and straight and quick-witted. A credit to Issa, he had always thought. His line. . . .

Issa pulled at his arm. "And you . . . you must never let Nithrin know that I told you. I want your oath on it."

He gave it, and Issa looked relieved, too. They walked together into the woods, Rowan shortening his stride to accommodate hers. "I'm on my way to see Rintu," he said. "Why don't you come with me?"

"I can't. I'm going to Nithrin's house—she wants me to look over her summer furs with her. She's expecting me." Happy pride shone from her eyes.

Rowan started to speak, but changed his mind. He had warned Issa often that Nithrin took advantage of her, but it was breath wasted. Besides, he knew himself how Nithrin's beauty could blind.

He thought back three cycles. Arak had been a late summer hatchling. So it must have been. . . .

He had no trouble remembering. He had gone to the muscale pond to bathe and had found Nithrin there, in full heat. She had been waiting for someone else, he suspected, but she had accepted him gladly. They had thrashed about in the reeds until the water was all brown mud, and not much later, on the bank, she had been ready again.

He had gone home to Linnit ashamed, but not enough to deter him from dreaming about future encounters.

There had been none. Nithrin had continued to treat him with the minimum of cold courtesy that she accorded to all members of Embri and Rintu's line except for Issa, who occupied a special niche as her adoring slave.

The trail branched, the broad fork leading to the dipu grove and the other, narrower one, into the isolated hollow where Rintu and Embri had settled after their return from exile.

Issa detained Rowan. "I'll need help again, if any of those hatchlings live. Who can I have this time?"

He considered. The older youngling house had no lack of volunteer keepers, but no one wanted the more exacting task of tending those newly out of the water. Dak and Vani had done it for two summers and Vani was egg-swollen again, but this time she intended to use a private pool and raise her offspring herself. Targ and Chula, who had served in the past, had their own young family now, and so did Nimo and Mogian. Any others who were free would be unlikely to agree, and he didn't like to bring pressure. "How about Orkas's pair?" he ventured. "They might be willing to try it, for the novelty if nothing else."

Issa groaned. "I'd rather have no one than those two. How could I trust them with new younglings when they can hardly look after themselves? No, I need someone responsible. I was thinking of Linnit. Would she do it, do you think?"

"I wouldn't want to ask her," Rowan said. He was surprised that Issa could be so insensitive.

She ignored his tone of rebuke. "Then I will. Linnit needs distraction right now, and what could be better than a house full of crying hatchlings?"

He set his mouth. "She won't do it."

"We'll see. Anyway, if this weather doesn't break, we may not even have a hatchling house." Issa rewrapped her mantle and hurried off, her short legs stumping purposefully.

Misdirected energy, Rowan thought. Nithrin would have her brushing and sewing until dark, when she should be overseeing the youngling house. Usually it was chaos without her. And as for thinking she knew what was best for Linnit—what a mistaken conceit.

Rowan followed a partially frozen path through a thicket of winter-dead seedfruit. Encroaching stalks whipped against his face, and he stopped to cut them back. He had never seen the trail so overgrown. Rintu must be too far along to work, he thought, and Embri unable to leave him. As he slashed at the underbrush, he upbraided himself for neglecting them. It had been far too long. . . .

The trail dipped, spanned a shallow stream set with stepping stones and rose again to disappear in the snow of a narrow clearing. Rowan was further disturbed when he saw that no smoke issued from the chimney of the squat stone house.

2

Embri, wrapped in furs, came to admit Rowan. Inside the
house, it was as cold as outdoors. The winter window stone
was in place and he could barely see, but he knew at once
what he would find. The fire pit appeared long unused, and
a sharp, briny odor permeated everything.

Rowan looked around for Rintu, and Embri pointed to the
darkest corner.

The bloated black form swathed in wet moss heaved itself
to a sitting position. Rowan went to him and stifled a gasp.
The eyes were the only features in the thick-skinned, lumpy
face that he could recognize as those of his egg-sire.

Rowan squatted beside the bulky shape. "Are you . . . all
right?" he asked, conscious as he spoke of the inanity of his
question. Rintu could barely move, and he wheezed with
every breath.

"I must . . . the water," he said in a rasping whisper. "Talk
to Embri. She won't—"

Embri hurried to Rintu and laid a finger on his mouth.
"No, it isn't time yet," she said firmly. "And don't try to

talk." She bathed his face from a bowl of seawater that contained floating greens, then held the container while he sucked up a mouthful.

She turned to Rowan. "I'll take him to the ocean when he's ready. But not yet. I can care for him here awhile longer." She sprinkled more water on the moss bed. "See how I've made him comfortable."

"Talk to her," Rintu repeated.

Rowan looked from one to the other. Rintu's eyes begged, and Embri's were anguished. "How can I let him go?" she said.

Rintu's gaze became unfocused. "Drifting," he whispered. "Yes, the greens . . . how they wave in the currents." He stared at a spot on the far wall. "The blue caves . . . the gardens in the rocks." He moved his grotesque head from side to side. "The singing. . . ."

He stared directly at Rowan. "They're waiting for me. So many. Waiting for me to sing."

"See: he doesn't know what he's saying," Embri said. "Tell him. Perhaps he'll believe *you*."

Rowan studied his sire, so grossly out of place in the stone house that was now a prison. "Why should I?" he countered. Embri was always so sure she was right. Why not leave Rintu with his illusions?

He had his answer. "You have to let him go," he said to her. "Soon he won't be able to breathe at all."

"I know." Embri's face was bleak. "But what will I do without him?"

He embraced her awkwardly. Embri had never been the one to need comfort. "You must think of yourself, too," he said. "You can't live like this, with no fire or hot food. You'll become ill."

She wrapped her outer fur more snugly. "I'm all right. He suffers, you know, if I have a fire." She bathed the exposed portions of Rintu's waterskin again, with a hand that to Rowan looked as thin and brittle as the winter branches he had cleared from the trail.

Rintu flopped and wheezed. Rowan wondered: in his

dreams, was he gliding sleekly through the water? As he watched the transformed creature labor, Rowan knew that Embri for once was wrong. Perhaps she didn't see an old one aching for his element when she looked at Rintu. Perhaps to her he was still the slender, handsome landling who had saved her with his cloak so long ago.

No, he couldn't blame Embri. But Rowan determined that Rintu, whatever it cost him, should have his final hours of waterlife.

"It *is* time," he said. "I'll get Dak and Nimo to help me, and we'll carry him to the beach."

"No, you can't...." Embri's protests followed him across the clearing, but he closed his ears.

The two egg-kin and their friend were silent as they left the beach. Rintu had slid into the waves as if he were going home, but they all knew that it would be a short return.

"I don't want to be the one to find him," Dak said when they were in the forest. His thin face was set tightly against emotion. "I'm not going near the beach for the next few days."

Rowan had made the same resolution. "I'll see that Embri keeps away, too," he said. "She can stay with Linnit and me for a while."

"I'll come look around tomorrow," Nimo offered. The stocky male was squint-eyed and ugly, but dependably kind. "It shouldn't be longer than that. I'll let you know."

Rowan made the sign of thanks. He parted from the others at Embri's trail, and as he descended into the hollow he planned what he would say to persuade her to leave with him.

He found Embri inside the house, crouched by the hearth. She had not made a fire or started to clean up the litter of moss and slimy seaweed that covered the floor. She did not look up at him or return his greeting, and when he led her out she offered no resistance.

Through the forest, she walked listlessly. Rowan attempted conversation on a variety of safe topics, but received no response. Finally he gave up. He should be grateful, he decided, that she was being so tractable; it was the last thing he had expected from her.

Linnit met them at the edge of their space, and Embri walked by her and into the house without a word.

Linnit stood rigid with fury.

"Don't be angry with her," Rowan pleaded. "She's just lost Rintu, and she's taking it hard."

Linnit waved aside his explanation. "Look," she said, pointing.

Rowan saw that Linnit's distress had nothing to do with Embri. The true cause was a jumbled heap of stones that was all that remained of her kiln.

"I just got back from the clay pit," Linnit said, "and that's what I found." She clenched and unclenched her fists. "It was Mim—I know it was. She'll pay for it, I promise! I'm going after her now."

The destruction shocked Rowan, too, but his immediate concern was to calm Linnit. "How can you be so sure?" he asked. "Why would Mim wreck the firebox when she could have used it as well? Perhaps it was some of the younglings —you know how wild they can get. I'll go see Issa and find out."

Linnit tightened her mouth. "It was Mim," she insisted. "She can't stand knowing that my pots are better than hers. I stopped by her house on my way to the pit and showed her the new ones, and you should have seen her face. I think she would have smashed the red bowl if I hadn't grabbed it away from her. Oh yes, it was Mim, all right."

"Then *I'll* go see her," Rowan said. "And don't worry about the firebox; we'll build another one."

Linnit was not mollified. "She invaded our space and destroyed our property. Just what exactly are you going to do about it?"

"Whatever is necessary," he said. "Trust me." Linnit's shoulders were taut to his touch as he turned her and led her toward the house. "I'll go now, if you promise to stay inside and talk to Embri. See if you can cheer her up, or at least get her to respond to something. I'm worried about her."

Linnit dipped her head. Rowan massaged the ridges of her neck until he felt her tension ease.

She gave him a half-ashamed smile. "I'm sorry—I wasn't listening before. Rintu's gone, you say? Of course, I'll do what I can for Embri." She shook off his hands and crossed the clearing in long-legged strides.

Mim lived on the lower spring trail, where it branched to the clay pit. It was a long walk, giving Rowan ample time to consider how to handle the difficult situation. It wasn't the first time the two potters had clashed. Linnit was never diplomatic, and Rowan had no doubts that she had flaunted her success. Still, Mim deserved more than a rebuke, but Rowan knew that anything he might do or say to her would only widen the breach between two who should be working together.

At times like this he wondered what he was doing as headman. It was supposed to be an honor, but he had never sought it or expected that it would ever be his. When he had been younger he had felt nothing but bitterness toward the tribe for injuries done to his kin. Now the tribe had taken over his life, to the extent of making him act the peacemaker between two touchy females. He sighed. It was an honor he could do well without.

Mim's clearing was slushy with fire-melted snow. A blackened circle marked the site of her recent burning, and the heap of broken pottery beside it spoke mutely of its failure.

Rowan called a greeting.

"You!" Mim peered through her doorflap. She squatted in the opening and stared at Rowan defiantly from across the tree space, making him wait long moments for a grudging permission to enter.

Rowan tried to summon all the authority of his position as he stood before her and returned her stare.

She averted her eyes first. "I know why you've come. It's Linnit, isn't it, crying over that thing she calls a firebox."

She looked up at him again, holding her back tree-straight. "Yes, I wrecked it. I have the right, as first potter. When she has fired clay as long as I have, then let her say how it should be done."

"No, you do not have the right," Rowan said sternly. "The firebox was in our space. You were always one of those who spoke the loudest about keeping the old patterns, so you should know what it is you have done."

"Oh, I know, and I'll starve for it if you choose to punish me that way. But I'll not build her another one, so save your breath if that's what you have in mind.

"Pagh!" She snorted and spat. "Yes, I raised my voice many times, and I was right. Covered fireboxes! Walled-in birthpools! Now we have a village overrun with screaming younglings who know nothing of proper respect. What does that Issa creature teach them, anyway? The other day a herd of them ran me off the path without even a sign of apology.

"Pagh! Fish-eating visitors who take our grain and our best hides. That shameless pair of Orkas's even mated with one, I hear. Imagine: a Sonsi hatchling in our birthpool! Lucky for us these hatchlings will all die.

"They will—everyone says so." She gave him a crafty look. "So what about me? Do anything you like. See—it doesn't matter now." She held up her hands, the four fingers joined halfway with thick, dark waterskin.

Rowan forced himself to remain impassive; he should have suspected. "I'll send you grain, Mim," he said. "Just stay away from Linnit, that's all." He made the farewell sign hastily and left the clearing, glancing, as he passed the fire circle, at the shards of broken clay. This time he took note of the coarseness and the uneven thicknesses. Picturing Mim's hands, he granted that she had ample cause for her bitterness.

Linnit agreed when he told her. He found her and Embri inside by the fire, deep in conversation. Whatever they were discussing, they stopped as soon as he came in. Linnit had a few sympathetic words to say about Mim; then she and Embri became bustlingly busy preparing a meal of baked tubers and watery grain mash. As the three of them ate, there was little talk.

No one mentioned Rintu. Rowan was relieved that Embri seemed to have come out of her initial shock. The tension in the atmosphere he attributed to her repressed grief. Awkward, but not unnatural.

Linnit spoke occasionally in monosyllables to Embri, but to Rowan she maintained the distance that had existed since the loss of the hatchling. The basket, Rowan saw, was gone from the corner.

The three slept far apart in the room. Rowan heard rain in the night, and toward morning he tossed aside his fur blanket. When he stepped outside at first light he felt the change. He walked across the clearing, whistling. The rain was soft, and there was no wind from the north.

"At last!" Linnit's voice came from behind him. He turned to share his pleasure with her, but she was already squishing through puddles back toward the house.

When Rowan entered, the two females looked up from a conspiratorial huddle. He had heard excited whispers, but his presence shut them off.

Let them have their secrets, he thought. He couldn't be bothered with such foolishness, with all he had to do now that the weather had broken. He swallowed a mouthful of cold mash and tied on thick footwraps.

It was good to be active again. With Dak and strong-shouldered Targ, their chief hunter, to help, Rowan tramped all the trails, distributing the last of the winter stores. As he did his visiting, he noted which houses were in most urgent need of repairs, heard a variety of complaints and organized a scouting party to search the outer forest for shurek signs. When the grain was gone, Dak and Targ went off on business of their own, and Rowan made a final call at the youngling house.

He found it warm and noisy with activity. At the far end of the long room Issa was leading her youngest charges in a sing, while near the door the guide Prem was readying the eight oldest for a foraging hike.

"Keep to the inner trails," Rowan warned. "The others aren't safe yet."

"I know." Prem passed out pouches and digging blades and short knives. He checked the footgear of each youngling and grunted his approval. "It may seem warmer, but there could still be snow in the high places, and once your toes are frostbitten. . . ."

The youngsters nodded solemnly. The tallest male had the clear, wide-spaced brown eyes that Rintu had passed on to his line. And now I to mine, Rowan thought.

Arak met Rowan's gaze. "You handle that well," Rowan said, indicating the knife that Arak twirled and sheathed in a single smooth motion.

Arak's pleasure showed in the flush that darkened his face. "Targ says I'm good with a spearshooter, too," he said. "He's promised to take me on his next hunt."

"Then I know what title to give you in the naming." Rowan smiled. It would give Nithrin pleasure too, he knew. If any hunter were to match Marek. . . .

"Oh, Rowan!" Issa called and beckoned. Prem left with his group, and Rowan crossed to the other end of the room.

"Could you stay here awhile?" Issa asked. She continued to mark the time with one hand while the little ones sang on their own. "Prem said he would send someone over, but I don't want to wait. I've got to see what's happening at the pool, and I haven't had a chance yet to talk to Linnit. You know—about the hatchling house. And—what do you think of this?—I thought I'd ask Embri, too. Wouldn't they make a great pair of tenders?"

"If they would do it," Rowan said. He thought: Embri, maybe, but not Linnit. But let Issa find out. "I'll stay, but not for long," he agreed.

The singing became more and more ragged, and finally it disintegrated into giggles and play. Issa put on her outside gear and Rowan shucked his off. A thick log burned in the pit, sending out too much heat. The younglings were dressed only in short singlets.

They numbered twelve, all well-formed except for one

with a scarred face and slightly misshapen legs. They should be strong, Rowan thought. These were the common hatchlings from the previous summer, the only survivors from countless clutches of eggs. Maybe it was pure chance that they were the ones to have overcome all the odds, but he didn't think so. He smiled as he watched them, content with what they boded for the future.

The play disintegrated into running and pushing and more shouting than Rowan could endure. He rounded up the darting figures and marched them around the room until they were happy to sit still. Fortunately, for he had no idea what to do next, Nimo's mate Mogian came in with her own hatchling in a basket.

"You! Prem didn't say I was to relieve the headman." She put down the basket and made a mock bow.

"Issa talked me into it. You know her."

"Rowan . . . Nimo said, if I were to see you . . ." Mogian bit her lip. She bent over the hatchling, adjusting something, before she continued. "He went to the beach this morning, and he found Rintu. Apparently he didn't last the night."

Tightness constricted Rowan's throat. He made the sign of thanks and then of leave-taking. Mogian nodded, and he retrieved his cloak. It had become a tent for two small hunters, and he left the house followed by their shrill protests.

He had intended to make one more journey to the meadow and the muscale pond, but he turned back when he found the low ground to be a morass of swamp. In any case, it was too early to tell what kind of seedgrass crop they could expect.

The rain continued as he trudged back to his clearing. No one was there, and the house was empty, too.

Linnit and Embri came in as he was making himself a meal. Both carried packs, which they set down inside the door. "Don't worry, I'm not moving in," Embri said. "I just went to my house to get some things we'll need for the trip."

"We . . . what trip?" Rowan looked from one to the other.

Embri went to the fire to warm her hands. Linnit added a

length of hide to her pack, then turned to Rowan. "Embri and I are going away," she said. Her face revealed nothing of what she might be feeling. "At least for the summer. Embri can't stay here where everything reminds her of Rintu, and I . . . I have my reasons for getting away, too.

"We're going to the grain valley. We'll do all the harvesting for the tribe, so if you send someone later, the seeds will be bagged and ready. Now that the weather's changed, we thought we'd leave right away.

"What do you think of the plan?" she asked as calmly as if she had been proposing a day's foraging.

3

"I think it's crazy! All that way. Across those mountains. Two females." Objections crowded Rowan's mind faster than he could spill them out. "It's through shurek country, and they'll be mean-hungry. Another thing—we haven't supplies to spare. And another—what would you live in? Neither of you is a builder. And you'd lose your summer eggtimes, both of you. Have you thought of that?"

Linnit continued to speak with calm resolution. "Yes, I've thought of it, and it's what I want. No more eggs and no more disappointments."

Embri turned from the fire. "That part of my life is over, too. I could never take another partner.

"And as for the dangers, you make too much of them. Dak and Prem have made the trip four times now. Perhaps you've forgotten that I've been in the wilds more than anyone. I'm not afraid. I'd go alone, but if Linnit wants to come, I'll be glad for her company."

"We won't take any food from the tribe," Linnit said. "We'll hunt as we go."

Rowan felt helpless in the face of such determination. But somehow he had to dissuade them. "Forget about the food," he said. "What about your work? I said I'd help you make a new firebox."

"It can wait. The tribe won't suffer for lack of a few pots."

He grew more desperate. "Perhaps not, but you *are* needed here, especially with the short summer we'll have. And all those hatchlings. Have you talked to Issa?"

"Yes, she told us her scheme." Linnit's mouth twisted in a wry grimace. "It's the last thing I'd want to do."

"Or me," Embri said. "Rowan, forget your own feelings for now. I know you don't want Linnit to leave, but try to think as a headman. We never have enough grain, and with a permanent settlement in the valley, we'd be assured of a steady supply."

"Permanent? But you said, 'just for the summer.'"

"I know, and we really haven't planned that far ahead. But we'll build a grain house—and I do know something about it after helping Rintu I don't know how many times."

Rowan acknowledged the truth in Embri's reasoning, but he could not rise above his personal hurt. He turned to Linnit again. "If it's me you want to get away from, why must you go so far? Do you think you wouldn't be safe from me in the village?"

"Not you. I wouldn't be safe from myself. Surely you can understand that."

He couldn't. It seemed to him that she was denying her nature, an affront to the tribe as well as to him.

Embri, too, was still fertile, though since Dak she had raised no live offspring. However, she had cause to isolate herself, Rowan granted. Linnit did not.

"So when do you plan to leave?" he asked coldly.

Embri answered, "In the morning. Early."

He relented enough to check their packs and offer them the last dried meat in the house, which Linnit accepted only when he threatened to throw it to the ergips. He went to bed early and pretended to sleep while the two females whispered, and at first light he awoke to find them dressed for the trail.

Linnit came to him. "Don't get up," she said. "And don't be angry for long. Or worry. You'll see, when you come for the grain, that Embri and I are made of strong stuff."

"And I *shall* miss you." For a moment, as she bent over him, Rowan thought she might touch him with her lips, their secret caress, but something in her eyes changed and she did not.

Embri shuffled her feet impatiently, and Linnit left Rowan to go to strap on her pack. They left, and Rowan wrapped himself in his blanket to watch them cross the clearing. They were two strangers, one tall and one short, swathed in furs. Linnit's black crest was flattened under her hood and her long-boned body was disguised by the bulky wrap, but when she turned to wave, the motion was so achingly familiar that he turned away with a curse.

Inside, he vented his anger by smashing Linnit's red bowl. He rolled up her bedding and the clothing that she had left behind, and then he was at a loss what to do with it. Finally he threw it in a corner. "Maybe you'll be back," he muttered, "but maybe, too, by then I won't be waiting."

He stared up at his headman's cape. He had been awarded it by acclaim, after Roko had died on the very journey that Embri and Linnit were now undertaking. There had been no other serious contenders, no one else who had the confidence of both the older landlings and the new breed.

He thought: what if someone from the tribe should see me now, throwing a tantrum like a youngling, all because a female has chosen to leave me. Embri was right—he should think and act like the headman he was. He swept up the pottery shards and buried them in the fire pit.

Rowan was kept too busy to mope in the ensuing days. Continuing heavy rain washed away the last vestiges of winter. Creeks overflowed, flooding low-lying houses, and a swollen sea inundated the birthpools. Chula and Vani lost their hatchlings, but Issa managed to save four from the common pool.

When the downpour finally stopped, the forest was renewed. Tender green growth appeared overnight on the dipus, and purple nodules covered the frangis. Brown winter bushes budded to life.

Rowan met in council at his house with Dak and Targ and Nimo to plan the major summer projects. In addition to the usual hunts and the one long trek to the grain valley, they had promised the Sonsi a trading expedition as soon as the weather settled. Broken Tree and two others from the starving southern tribe had made a winter crossing of the lava, begging help. Rowan had given them what grain he could spare, agreeing to defer payment until summer.

"You're sure you can make it on those floating logs of yours?" Rowan asked Nimo. "That's a rough sea on that stretch of coast."

"I only have to go by water past the black rocks," Nimo said. "And yes, I've tested the raft often enough. Once I get it beyond the breakers I'll be all right."

"Who will you take with you?"

Nimo's squinting eyes were lost in folds of flesh. "I had planned on asking Embri—she's the only one of us who can talk to them. But since she's gone, it can be anyone. How about you, Dak?"

"Sure. I know a few Sonsi words, and I'd like to learn more. But I can't go until after Vani's next heat. She wants to try for another hatchling, a late summer one."

"Forget it, then," Nimo said. "I can't make plans around something like that." He turned to the hunter. "Targ? Would you like to come?"

"Yes, but . . ." Targ shifted uneasily. "I have the same problem as Dak. Chula . . ."

Nimo groaned.

"Why not take the females along?" Rowan suggested. "Issa can see to the younglings."

Nimo considered, and nodded. "I can take three on the raft. Dak—you and Vani?"

"Agreed." They sealed it with crossed hands.

"We can talk about the trade goods later," Rowan said. "Let me know when you're ready to leave."

"Of course that means I won't be able to go after the grain," Dak said. "But Prem knows the way as well as I do. He can take one of the new trailmakers. They have to learn."

"They won't have to stay long," Rowan said. "If Embri and Linnit got through all right, they'll have the grain ready. The four can come back together."

Rowan guarded himself when he spoke of Linnit, but he was conscious of a rush of heat that threatened to betray him. Her desertion still rankled. Chula and Vani hadn't let disappointment defeat them, he thought. Granted, they had other younglings while Linnit didn't. But even so, for her to give up so entirely . . . he didn't know if he would ever feel the same about her.

"Too bad you let those two go," Nimo said. "In my opinion, it was a foolish risk. With so many old ones lost this winter, we ought to be more careful. Two females, especially."

Rowan rose. "I didn't ask for your opinion," he said curtly.

Targ glanced up at Rowan and made a gesture of sympathy. "I'm sorry about Rintu," he said. "It's hard, I know. Suri has started the change, too, and already Chula is worrying herself more than she should. Perhaps it's just as well Linnit isn't here."

"So I thought." Rowan seized gratefully on the face-saving lie.

Nimo looked ashamed and murmured an apology.

"Forget it," Rowan said. He tried to do so as well, as they continued the meeting with routine hunting assignments and with plans for the upcoming naming ceremony.

When they left, the house was too empty. Rowan ate a cold meal and went to bed before it was dark.

He hated the house now, as he did the fire-marked clearing, and arranged to be away as much as possible. He went on hunts and cleared trails and spent hours assisting the new initiates with their shelters.

Arak had chosen to build in the Sonsi manner, a round house of wood blocks and baked clay. Rowan helped him to erect and brace the beams, but the infilling the young landling did himself.

He worked with care and precision, Rowan noted with pride. And displayed cleverness, too. As he built up the walls he added unique touches such as grauf bones for hangers and a translucent shell that let in light.

Rowan came often to watch and encourage, and one morning, so did Nithrin.

She was more beautiful than ever. Maturity had rounded and softened the contours of her body without destroying their supple tone. Her face showed no traces of age, and her crest still flamed.

Rowan would have liked to know her thoughts as she regarded Arak, but her expression was unreadable. Her relationship to her two egg-issue had always been curious. The first, a female of now some nine cycles, she barely acknowledged and never visited. She had not done so even when the scrawny, wizened youngling had been in Issa's care. Grown, her looks had not improved, and Nithrin had waited a long time before using a private pool again.

Arak, however, had turned out more to her liking. She had come to see him frequently in the youngling house, petting him and leaving Issa to deal with tears and temper when she left. It was a wonder, Rowan thought, that Arak had grown up to be so pleasantly disposed.

Arak stopped his work when he saw Nithrin. "Come, let me show you what I've done," he said. He took her arm as carefully as if she were a treasure and led her inside the half-walled structure. "It's going to be much higher than the Sonsi houses," he explained. "See, these beams will make it stronger. Feel the walls, how smooth they are. I may not even use hides, at least not all around. See the pretty stones I've set in. What do you think?"

Nithrin dutifully touched the walls. She appeared puzzled

by the strangeness. "I like hides," she said. "They're soft and warm."

Some of the brightness left Arak's eyes. "Then I'll use them," he said. "The walls will be black anyway after the fire."

Rowan stepped foreward. "Arak has a gift for building. For one so young, what he has done here is remarkable."

Nithrin shot him a look of displeasure. "Arak is a hunter," she said. "This"—she waved her hand disparagingly—"this is work anyone can do."

"Not anyone." Rowan would have said more, but he saw that she took increasing exception to his words.

"Arak's title has been decided," she said coldly. "He chose it himself, and I agree."

"Yes, yes, and I don't want to change anything." Arak's anxious eyes were on Nithrin. "This"—he imitated her gesture—"is just play."

Nithrin smiled, and Arak lost his tenseness. "I'm going with Targ and the others tomorrow," he said. "After twinhorns. I'll bring you a trophy, I know I will."

"I'm sure of it." She reached out with her hand to touch his cheek, but checked herself. "You'll need the horns, though, for your doorway. That's where Marek kept his, up there." She pointed, and Arak nodded.

Rowan waited on the trail for Nithrin to finish her visit. He had to talk to her about Arak. He thought of himself and Rintu, their closeness when he had been Arak's age, and it was bitter to him that he was being denied the same rights and pleasures.

It wasn't fair to Arak, either. He regretted his promise to Issa, and though he knew he could never break an oath, he hoped that he might be able to force an admission from Nithrin that would free him.

Nithrin was not long with Arak. Her eyes widened when she saw Rowan, but she accompanied him willingly along the trail. "I've been wanting to talk to you, too," she said.

"About Arak?"

She started. "No, why would you think that?"

"Because of the way you acted back there. I thought you might accuse me of trying to influence him away from the course you've set for him. There's nothing wrong with his interest in building, no matter how mighty a hunter he might be. If he should ever become headman, he would need to know many skills."

"Do you think it's possible? That he would be headman someday?"

Rowan laughed. "Don't pretend. I know it's been in your mind all along. And yes, I do think it's possible. I intend to be around for some time yet, but Arak shows more promise than any of the young ones."

"You'll . . . take an interest in him? See that he learns what he should?"

He watched her intently. "If you can give me a good reason. I have many claims on my time, you know."

Nithrin stiffened and slowed her stride. "What do you mean, 'good reason'?" Her eyes met Rowan's uneasily, then looked quickly away. "I should think you'd want to help him, for the sake of the tribe. I should think it would be important to train a likely successor."

"No one did it for me."

She grew more agitated. "We're not talking about the past!"

"Then why are you so frightened?" He guessed the reason: that old business with Rintu and Marek. She was afraid he might tell Arak of her past if he knew the youth as his issue.

He had to put her at ease if he were to get the admission he sought. "I would never tell Arak anything that would cause him to think less of you," he said. He ventured more. "Whatever you may have done once to Rintu—it's long forgotten."

"You don't know anything anyway! You never did!"

"Of course not. You're the only one who knows the truth."

"Then let's forget it. Why are we talking like this, anyway? All because I asked you to take a headman's interest in Arak."

He took advantage of her confusion. "Only a headman's?"

"Issa told you!"

"She told me nothing. I guessed."

"Say it, then."

"If you wish. Ours. Our issue. Yours and mine."

She still looked frightened, but whatever she saw in Rowan's face apparently reassured her. "Yes, it's true," she said.

"Why didn't you want me to know?"

She looked at the ground. "There was Linnit. . . ."

It wasn't the real reason, he knew. Nithrin would never have considered the feelings of one who meant nothing to her. No, it wasn't hard to imagine her motives. She had wanted to pretend that the youngling was Marek's.

"Will you tell Arak?" Rowan asked.

Nithrin frowned, a dark crease marring the smooth perfection of her brow. "What would be the point now? He couldn't keep the secret, and do you really want everyone to know? Linnit, when she returns?" She scuffed her foot in the dirt.

Such a small, narrow foot. Linnit's were huge by comparison. "She may not return," Rowan said. "But you're right; there's no need to reveal it now. No one will question the time I spend with a promising new tribe member."

Her brow cleared. "Then that's settled." She managed a shaky laugh. "Now, what was it I wanted to see *you* about?"

He smiled. "Your roof is leaking? You've had a shattering vision?"

His lightness brought an answering pout. "You don't think my farseeings are of much importance, do you? Nothing but fancies." Her lips tightened. "Perhaps I won't tell you, after all."

"No, I don't think that. I never have." Why was she so sensitive? "Your visions have always helped us. Everyone knows it. Now tell me: what have you seen?"

She relented. "Come with me, then. I'll show you."

He followed her, back to the main trail and then down toward the meadow. She walked fast, with a fluid motion that did not sacrifice speed to dignity.

The first tender growth of tallgrass covered the meadow, a pale green blanket interspersed with early wildflowers and the darker shade of a different kind of sprouts. "Over there," Nithrin pointed and led the way to a patch of the unfamiliar, round-leafed plants. She dropped to a squat and carefully uprooted one of the smallest sprouts. She brushed off the dirt and presented it to Rowan. "There—the white seed. See how the plant grows from it."

Rowan examined it curiously. "It looks like the ones in the Sonsi seedpods. Perhaps someone dropped it here at the last feast."

"Lots of them, remember? Those younglings tore the sack open and ran off with handfuls. Issa had to chase them all over the meadow."

"Yes, I remember it now." Rowan dug up more sprouts, the smaller ones all containing the remnant of a seed. "How did you find this?"

"I told you, I had one of my farsights. It was here in the meadow, and I saw into the earth and what was growing from the seeds.

"I saw these podplants first, because they were the biggest, but I also saw the tallgrass coming out of smaller seeds. The same ones that we gather and cook."

Rowan pulled up handfuls of tallgrass, but the roots were clean. "Are you sure?" he asked.

"Don't you believe me? I tell you I saw it. It was this many days ago"—she held up a hand—"and these grasses have already eaten up the seed. But they started from it, just like the podplants."

Implications flooded in upon Rowan. Could they do it themselves? No more dependence on the scant crop of the meadow for grain, or on long trips to the valley beyond the mountains. Or to the Sonsi for whitepods. No more winter hunger.

One step at a time, he told himself. He would try it first, in his own clearing. Then, if it worked. . . .

He forgot propriety and embraced Nithrin.

She didn't appear to be offended, though she pushed him away. "So you think I'm of some worth, after all?" she said, smiling. "Roko did, you know. But you—you have your own councils, and it seems they don't need a farseer."

He didn't know what to say. Admit her to his inner circle? He had often thought of inviting Issa, but she was always so busy. He didn't know how Nimo and Targ would react to Nithrin. Dak hated her, having listened much to Embri.

Nithrin shrugged. "It's all right; I understand. Perhaps Arak will need me someday, if it works out the way we hope."

"Yes, and I'll do all I can to see that it does." He liked the warmth that came to him when he and Nithrin spoke of their common issue. He knew now that when he had pressed her for an admission, it had as much to do with Nithrin as with Arak; he had wanted the acknowledged bond between them.

Nithrin looked toward the pond and smiled again. He ventured a guess as to her thoughts. "Do you remember?"

This time, she allowed his embrace.

4

Nithrin came to Rowan in her next heat, as he had hoped she would. They spent an entire afternoon inside his house with the doorflaps fastened, talking and laughing and eating between mating bouts that made all of his previous experiences seem pale. Rowan had never been so proud in his maleness. Nithrin's naked beauty inflamed him even when her scent was low, and when it returned each time stronger, he felt more than mortal.

They spoke only nonsense throughout the hours—endearments and loving taunts and murmurs of praise. Nithrin was like a youngling, freed from her usual proud constraints. She ate briny seagreens from his fingers and giggled at the mess, and dared him to pursue her in silly games; and always, when she grew most excited, the musk would arise to engulf them both.

Rowan could think of nothing but the moment. Later, he assumed, there would be time for serious talk and for plans. He knew only that his life would never be the same.

He was jolted when Nithrin left him at dusk, as casually

as if she had merely dropped in for klava. She picked up her furs and dressed, said a polite good-bye and was gone before he could gather his wits.

He knew it was the old way. Indeed, she had acted the same after their one previous mating. But this, he thought, had been different. They had shared something too exceptional for her to pretend it had never happened.

He wouldn't let her, he decided. This time he would determine the course of their relationship. He knew all her faults—better than anyone, perhaps. But still he couldn't get her out of his thoughts. He pictured her as he had seen her in a hundred guises: swathed in heavy furs, waiting out the winter with dreamy patience; stripped to her tunic at a feast, grease-stained and greedy; laughing with Cuma, condescending with Issa; fierce over Arak and always, in whatever posture, imbued with the luminous quality that made every other female appear drab.

He knew how she had ruled Roko, but he had no fears for himself—he could never be so subjugated. Nor was he concerned about what others might think. It was his life, and he wanted Nithrin in it with him as he had lived with Linnit, sharing more than an occasional rutting.

He approached her about it the next day, at a time when she was alone in her clearing. She sat bent over a bit of sewing, her crest burnished by slivers of sun that winked through the arching dipus.

She saw him and waved him in. "Arak should return from his hunt today." She held up the ornamental band she had been stitching: bright shells against snowy fur. "It's for his horns. I know he'll get them this time."

Arak had had bad luck on his first two hunts, unable to get a shot. This time Targ had promised him a lead position, and Rowan, too, expected a good report.

But he hadn't come to discuss Arak. "Why did you leave me so suddenly yesterday?" he asked as he squatted beside her. "We should have talked. There are many things I wanted to say to you."

She moved away from him as she reached for a sewing

prick, and settled herself at the new distance. "I'm listening," she said. "What was it you wanted?"

He searched her face for a trace of what they had shared. It was hard to believe that she could be so changed. Surely, he thought, some feelings must carry over, as they did for him.

It was awkward, with no encouragement, but he plunged ahead. "It seemed to me . . . after the happiness we gave each other . . . we should be more to each other than before. I'd like nothing better than to see you every day, to be with you. . . ."

"You see me now," she said.

"You know what I mean. To share a house, to be there for all your ruttings."

She stood up, spilling her shells onto the ground. "You insult me, headman," she said.

"I didn't mean to."

"Then you know nothing of true landlings." She made the sign of dismissal and waited stiffly for him to leave, and he could do nothing else.

He hurried through the dipus, circling off-trail to keep from meeting anyone. He should have foreseen Nithrin's reaction, he thought in his anger and shame. He had assumed too much from a few hours of irrational pleasure.

Only she could have made him act like such a fool. He reviewed everything unfavorable he knew about her: her pride and her selfishness and the harm she had done by her scheming ways. It helped to restore his judgment, though he admitted to himself that he would forgive her everything if she were to call him back.

She didn't, and he emerged from her grove with his own pride still bruised. Later in the day, with a cooler head, he wondered what he would have done if she had accepted and if Linnit had then returned to him. Would he have been prepared to make a choice?

No, it was for the best, he admitted, though the rejection continued to gall. He would see Nithrin enough, through Arak, and in all probability they would have other matings.

*   *   *

The hunt was successful. Targ's band brought in two grauf, a twin and a single-horn, but neither was killed by Arak's hand.

The young hunter would not look at Rowan when the meat was presented and the horns awarded, and after the ceremony he went directly to his house, leaving the klava and the stories to others in the party.

Targ looked after him with worried eyes.

"He missed his shot," said the other neophyte, Alloran, the one who had won the horns. "We would have lost the grauf if I hadn't thrown, too. And I had only a long spear while Arak had the shooter."

"I can't understand it," Targ said. "In all the practices, Arak was dead on target. He has a better eye than anyone; it's why I let him use the shooter."

"He missed on purpose," said Damin, the oldest on the team. "He froze when he saw the grauf. "I've seen it happen before, and the one it happened to was no use ever as a hunter."

Rowan sighed. At the naming, he had given Arak the title he wanted, though he personally would have preferred the youth to focus his talents in other directions. There were many choices. The tribe had an abundance of hunters, but only two healers, Suri and Chula, and now Suri would be gone soon. Arak had mastered the tally sticks with unparalleled ease, and Rowan had in mind a new position, a keeper of stores and records, that would lighten much of his own work load. And if he chose, the young landling could easily surpass his own or even Rintu's achievements as a builder.

But he had wanted only to hunt. Rowan made a division of the meat, and as soon as his guests left, he hurried to Arak's house.

He was admitted grudgingly. Arak crouched by the hearth, staring into a dead fire. "I suppose you've heard," he said.

Rowan's throat tightened in pity, but he was careful to

keep it from his voice. "Targ was on at least four hunts before he got his horns. Maybe it was more, I forget. Ask him sometime."

"I've heard that story." Arak still did not look up. "The older hunters wouldn't give him a shot. But that wasn't the case with me—I had the best chance of all."

"What happened, then?" Rowan lowered himself to sit beside the stiff figure.

"I couldn't shoot. I had a line on him, right between the eyes, and my shortspear ready with the cord pulled tight and I couldn't shoot. That grauf looked at me and I let the spear go way beyond him, anywhere, and he started to run and Alloran got him in the flank."

"What did Targ say?"

"Just 'bad luck'; you know how he is. But Damin—he told me I'd better learn to dry fruit or make baskets." The voice was heavy with misery. "Maybe you think so, too."

"You know better than that. Look around at this house if you're beginning to doubt your own worth. Hunting isn't everything."

"To me it is!" Arak jumped up and began to pace. "I'll do better next time, I know I will. It was just the surprise, seeing a live target. You don't think Targ will refuse to take me anymore, do you?"

"No, not if you're still serious in your calling," Rowan said. "If you're sure."

"I am! It's all I've ever wanted, to be a hunter."

Or that Nithrin wanted, Rowan said to himself. She was the only one who could ever dissuade Arak, and it was doubtful that she would.

He got up to leave. "You'll come by to help me mark down the meat shares?" he asked.

"No, I won't have time," Arak said. "I've got to practice a lot more with the long spear—it's probably what I'll be using next time." He grimaced. "I know I won't be getting another chance with the shooter."

* * *

Rowan spent an inordinate amount of time worrying about Arak. It was not what he had expected from their relationship; Arak's single-mindedness allowed for none of the guidance that Rowan had been prepared to offer. Nevertheless, he had to admire the youth for his perseverance. He observed him often at his spear practice, first in his own clearing, alone, and then at Targ's with the other young hunters.

Arak appeared to have suffered no loss of confidence. He aimed and threw again and again, his skin glistening and the muscles on his arms and shoulders strongly defined, challenging the others to greater distances.

Thunk! Thunk! Thunk! A barrage of spears hit the target tree. "You did it again!" someone shouted as Arak's proved closest to the mark.

"Another five paces. Anyone." Arak waved his spear when he saw Rowan, and the headman watched him win another challenge.

Targ, who was overseeing the practice, made a sign of approval.

"He's certainly recovered from his first failure, hasn't he?" Rowan said.

"He's determined," Targ agreed. "If that means anything, he'll make it yet as a hunter."

"Then you don't believe what Damin said?"

"I just don't know. I've heard that story, too. It was Nols he was talking about, and Damin claims that's the reason he turned to klava."

"Fah! Nols was always a weakling. Nothing like Arak, there."

"That's why I won't make any predictions," Targ said. "I'm taking the whole band out soon, so we'll see."

Chula came out of the house with a youngling clasped firmly by one hand. In the other she carried a food basket. "Targ!" she called. "Make them stop that so we can get through to the trail. I'm going to Suri's."

Targ signaled a halt to the practice, and Chula crossed the clearing.

Rowan took leave of Targ and hurried after her. "How is Suri?" he asked.

"As well as you could expect. She wouldn't take her share of the meat—says it's ridiculous to waste good food on her."

"But isn't she always hungry?"

"She won't admit it. She's trying to hold off this thing as long as she can, but I think she's only damaging herself faster."

The youngling began to whimper. "Wha's w'ong wi' Suri?" she lisped.

Chula picked her up, hooking the basket over her arm. "She's changing, like I told you. Like Pellen did when we saw her swim away."

The youngling cried harder and tried to wriggle out of Chula's arms. "I don' wanna see Suri," she sobbed.

As they started up the trail to Suri's grove, Chula looked at Rowan with a worried frown. "She's so frightened, I don't know if I should . . ."

"It's all right," Rowan said. "You go on, and I'll take her back to Targ. I'll visit Suri some other time."

Chula transferred her burden to Rowan. "I thought she should learn about it early, but now I'm not so sure it was wise."

Rowan shared her perplexity. "I can't remember how I first found out, but I know it was a shock the first time I saw an old one. How does Issa handle it?"

"She puts it in her songs." Chula wrinkled her nose. "I can't sing—I have nothing but a squawk. But say—drop Kalina off at the youngling house and ask Isa to be sure to have a song session. Tell her what kind." She was off.

"And say"—she turned and called over her shoulder—"when are you going after Linnit?"

Chula apparently did not expect an answer—she was already out of sight—but Rowan wondered what had prompted the question. She knew that there would be no mountain crossing until the grain was ripe, and he had never thought to go himself. Had there been talk already about him and Nithrin?

He discarded the idea. Nithrin was too circumspect to inspire gossip. Probably Chula just wanted Linnit around to help her with Suri.

Linnit had been inconsiderate to leave Chula with all the burden. But perhaps she hadn't known about Suri, she had been so absorbed in her own concerns.

Kalina snuggled a wet face into Rowan's shoulder. If she could have been theirs, he thought, his and Linnit's. He had never held Arak as a youngling and he ached for the loss.

5

Arak, for all his practicing, did no better on his next hunt. He threw wildly at a tusker and almost injured his own stalking partner.

Targ was coldly furious. He came to Rowan with no meat and harsh words about the hunter at fault. "I have no more time to waste on that one," he said. "He's worse than a bungler—he's dangerous. If he goes out again, it won't be with me."

Rowan had no choice but to deny the youth the hunting trails. When he went to tell him, Arak appeared too miserable to care. "Does Nithrin know?" was all he said. The words were forced from between tight-clamped teeth.

"I haven't told her," Rowan assured him. "Perhaps you should."

Arak shook his head mutely.

"Do you want me to do it?"

The youth assented with a choking grunt.

Rowan ached for his pain, but the only kindness he could

do Arak was to make a quick exit, leaving him to suffer without a witness.

Nithrin, he found, had already heard. "Damin came by with his 'I-told-you-so's,'" she exclaimed. "How I hate that smug-faced liar!" She had all her wall hangings outside on bushes and trees, and she swiped angrily at them with a frangi bough.

"But it wasn't a lie." Rowan held her by the arm. "Look at me, Nithrin. You have to face it: Arak is no hunter."

She pulled herself free. "Damin said he was a coward. I'll never believe that. Never." Her teeth were as tightly clamped as Arak's had been. She attacked a chula skin, sending up clouds of dust.

"I agree. Arak is no coward." Rowan followed her about the clearing as she continued thumping the skins. "Damin is a fool. Arak has no blood-lust, and that's all he lacks. It has nothing to do with courage. There are others, too, who have to steel themselves to kill. Nimo, for instance—it's why he never goes out with the band. Everyone knows it, and they don't think any less of him."

His words appeared to make no impression. Doggedly, Nithrin continued her work.

Rowan lost his patience. "Stop that and listen to me!" he shouted. "We have to think how we can help him. We have to do it together."

She put down the bough. Her face was without beauty, worn and bleak. "What can I do now? Everything has failed."

Don't you know? he wanted to scream at her. As Arak's egg-source, she shouldn't need anyone to tell her how to comfort him.

Nithrin stared vacantly, and Rowan held himself in check. She was of the old kind, he reminded himself. And she had never been a tender. When he spoke, it was with no rancor that could offend her. "I think Arak is more sick about what you will think about him than anything else."

She did not react.

"Tell him that it doesn't matter," he went on. "Tell him

that you still value him, care for him, even if he isn't a mighty hunter like Marek. That's what he needs to hear— that you haven't given him up because one particular plan didn't work out. He's so clever, and there are so many other things he can do. Do better than anyone. He can still be headman someday. Wait and see: everyone will forget about this."

Nithrin clenched and unclenched her fists as her eyes bulged. Rowan realized that she had heard nothing of what he was saying; she was in the grip of one of her spells. She made a gurgle deep in her throat, opened her mouth and fell to the ground.

Rowan ran for the water jar and bathed her face. Her hands were icy, and he warmed them in his. He thought of going for Chula, but he was afraid to leave. In any case, he knew that Nithrin preferred privacy during her attacks; she would not thank him for bringing help.

When she began to breathe noisily, taking in air in great choking gasps, Rowan helped her to sit. Gradually the stiffness left her limbs and her eyes focused again.

She looked at him with frightened recognition. "What did I do? Did I say anything?"

"No, nothing. You were like someone dead. Are you all right now? What can I get you?"

"A drink of klava. The jar is just inside the door. And hand me one of those furs." She clutched her arms and shivered.

Rowan dragged a skin from the nearest bush and wrapped her in it. He hurried into the house and found the jar.

When he came back with the klava, Nithrin appeared composed. She sipped, and her normal color returned. "They come most often when I'm troubled," she said. "I should have expected it, I was so upset about Arak."

She didn't seem troubled now. "What did you see?" Rowan asked.

She smiled and gave no answer.

He repeated the question.

"Nothing . . . that is, nothing important," she said. "Nothing that I need to tell you." She passed him the jar. "Please, don't think me rude. I know you came here for Arak's sake, and I thank you for it. But you must not worry about him any longer."

"Then you will talk to him? Tell him that you aren't angry with him?"

"Angry? Of course I'm not angry. Arak will be fine. He'll be . . ." She caught herself and stopped. "Yes, I'll talk to him. I'll go right away."

She started to get up, but Rowan pulled her back. "Wait at least until you feel stronger. It will give Arak time to get over his first shame. I don't think he wants to see anyone now."

"He'll see me."

Rowan released her and she rose, swaying at first. A fine rain started, but she showed no concern for her exposed hides. As soon as she was steady on her feet, she was out of the clearing.

Whatever Nithrin said to Arak, Rowan was relieved that it seemed to help. Arak stayed in his house for two days, and when he came out he was changed. His confident, exuberant manner was gone, but neither was he afraid to face others. His disgrace was the talk of the tribe for a handspan of days, until more immediate concerns put it in the background.

As the days of the short summer flew by, Rowan was as busy as every other adult in the tribe—hunting or digging tubers or picking berries or diving for mussels. Mogian put up her drying racks, and they began to fill.

The bed of seedpods and tallgrass in Rowan's clearing came up, but the plants were spindly and he despaired of ever planting enough to make the labor worthwhile. And where in the forest, he wondered, was there enough space? He still saw promise in the idea, but he put it aside for another season.

He saw Nimo and Dak and Vani off on their trading venture to the Sonsi. The raft would be launched from the sea-

green cove—another first. The tallgrass in the meadow
grew chest high and turned golden, and Prem began to prepare for his journey, too.

Then, when Rowan believed the summer would pass
safely and with the tribe well-provisioned, a band of shureks
invaded the outer trails. Prem and two neophyte trailmakers
were attacked near the high spring. Prem was injured and
one of his young companions was killed. There could be no
more hunting until the beasts were driven off; and worse,
there was no one to go for the winter grain.

Rowan weighed duty against his inclinations. He wasn't
ready to see Linnit, but it seemed there was no other choice
unless Prem made a miraculous recovery.

He went to visit the trailmaker at Suri's house. He lay
propped up on a wooden rack, his left leg and thigh bound
with strips of hide and covered with gourd-leaf poultices.
His face was drawn, but it had no feverish spots. His eyes
were sunken, but clear.

Suri watched over the wounded male. Well into the
change, she walked now with difficulty, and Rowan wondered how she could manage such a patient. "Where is
Chula?" he asked.

"She'll be back," Prem said. "She had to see about something at her own house. But don't worry; Suri has plenty of
help here."

The doorflap opened and Arak came in with a handful of
pungent-smelling leaves. He showed them to Suri. "Are
these the right ones?" When he noticed Rowan, he drew
back.

Rowan and Arak exchanged the shortest of polite greetings. Suri watched while Arak added the leaves to a brew
that was simmering over the fire. She sniffed, signaled for a
taste, and nodded. Arak withdrew to stand in a shadowed
corner by the door.

He should know that I approve of what he is doing,
Rowan thought. Yet Arak excused himself and hurried out as
soon as he could decently do so, as if to escape any chance
of a private conversation.

"Too bad about that one," Prem said as soon as the door-flap settled.

Rowan frowned, troubled that Arak might have heard. "There's been enough talk," he said. "I don't want to listen to any more." He settled himself near Prem. "I came to find out how you were—if you'll be able to travel at all this season." He glanced at the heavily poulticed leg. "It doesn't look like it."

Suri approached with a bowl of her brew, but Prem waved her back. "Later." He turned to Rowan. "No, Chula says I'm off my feet until midwinter. Have you talked to Biku? He might be willing to make the mountain crossing. I can't think of anyone else except Targ, and of course he'll be busy now hunting down shureks."

"No, Targ can't go. And Biku doesn't want to. He's only made the trip once, and he claims he can't remember the way. I think he's afraid because of the shureks acting up. But whatever the reason, he won't go unless he has a partner he can rely on."

"Who?" Prem looked up at Rowan. "Oh, you're thinking of going yourself?"

Rowan shrugged. "I don't like to leave now, but we can't do without the grain. Targ can take care of things here. I came to get the directions from you, in case Biku really does have such a bad memory."

"Oh, he knows the route, all right. But here, let me draw you a map." Prem reached for a stick of charcoal and Rowan removed the hides from a spot on the floor.

As Prem explained, Rowan memorized the drawing. He was no trailmaker, but he knew he could surely make the journey as well as two females.

If they had succeeded, that is. He was about to find out.

6

Rowan and Biku looked down upon the valley. It lay shimmering golden in the late afternoon sun, an expanse of grain that extended as far as Rowan could see, to the mountains beyond.

Enough to feed any number of tribes, he thought. Only a fraction had been cut, tiny brown squares beside the stream. In one of the squares, he saw what looked like a pebble and guessed it to be Embri and Linnit's hut.

"We can never make it down before dark," Rowan said. He would have liked to push on, but his better sense warned him against getting caught in twilight in shurek-infested country.

"Another hour," Biku suggested. He was as eager as Rowan to get out of the mountains. "We'll stop early and make a big fire."

Biku had been a nervous traveling companion, sure that every unfamiliar howl betokened a band of ravening beasts. Their one sight of shureks, at a distance enabling them to flee safely, had convinced him that the hairy ones were hiding in every thicket.

"Whatever made you decide to be a trailmaker?" Rowan asked as they shouldered their packs and started out again.

Biku was short and stocky, with a mouth that drooped on one side. He was heavy-footed for a forest walker. "A stupid choice, wasn't it?" He spat in disgust. "But as a youngling, it sounded exciting. Then, when I found out what it was really like, I was too ashamed to quit. Even knowing I was risking my hide every time I went out, I was more afraid of Dak and Prem and what they would think." He eyed a steep decline covered with loose rubble, tested it with his foot and slid clumsily down.

Rowan followed in a cascade of stones.

"This will be my last trip, though." Biku joined two fingers in the sign of promise. "If we make it back."

They stopped to shake out their footwraps. The valley was hidden now by a series of ridges, sparsely wooded on the high ground where they stood, but solidly green on the downward slopes.

Rowan did not share Biku's obsessive fears. Neither did he suffer from any of the claustrophobic reactions that Rintu had once described to him. He found the interior forest no more menacing than the one that bordered the ocean. And the valley that he had glimpsed—ah, he could live there, he thought.

Biku slowed his headlong pace when they entered thicker cover. The light failed quickly, and he selected a campsite in an area more open than most.

Rowan stared into the fire and allowed himself at last to think of Linnit. He had tried to keep the meeting out of his mind during the journey, and now that he was faced with it, he had no idea what to expect. Or even what he wanted. He still harbored bitter feelings, and of course there was now Nithrin.

And there was Arak, too. Whatever happened, Rowan knew that he and Linnit could never return to the same uncomplicated relationship they had once shared.

Biku was quiet for a long time, too. The fire cast a warm glow, and in its protective circle both males ventured confidences. Biku spoke of what he had expected from the trails and how he had been disillusioned, and Rowan of his hopes when he had become headman, his dreams of winters without hunger and a tribe that would increase and spread through the forest.

"We haven't done so badly," Biku said. "We're better off than in Roko's time."

Rowan threw a cone and watched the embers flare. "Rintu used to talk of such plenty."

"That! Do you really believe those old ones' stories?"

"Why should they lie?"

"Maybe they don't mean to. You know yourself how much better everything seemed when you were a youngling."

"Not for me. I was an outcast. We all were: Embri and Rintu and Issa and I. When I was small, no one but my egg-kin would have anything to do with me."

"Why ever not?"

Though Biku was an adult of some six cycles, it seemed to Rowan that he was the most untaught of younglings. "Because I was . . . unnatural," Rowan said. "Didn't you learn anything from Issa's songs?"

"I don't believe everything in them, either. Who is there here who can say that he spent all of his youngling years in the ocean?"

"Many, though they don't often speak of it. Suri, Nols, Embri, Nithrin, Cuma. Ask Embri when we see her."

Biku said no more, but by the set of his mouth, Rowan knew that he persisted in his doubts.

The two broke camp early in the morning, and by high sun they were in the valley. However, the cleared field proved to be farther away than it had appeared from on the mountain. Biku led the way along the stream, first through a marshy area of sedge, and then, on dry ground, through a tangle of tallgrass grain mixed with thistles and sticky webvines.

Gradually the grain crowded out the intruding growth, and the headway was easier. The brittle stalks were taller than any Rowan had seen, and heavy with heads of ripe seeds. Abruptly they gave way to a field that had been cut.

The hut stood in the middle of the field. It was low, with brown earthen walls and roof. Though it and the clearing appeared deserted, Rowan remained at the outer edge and shouted; it was, after all, a private space.

There was no answer. He nodded to Biku and they walked on over the stubble.

Inside, the hut was dug out below the level of the ground. It contained nothing but bags of grain piled against the walls and two untidy nests of bedding. Outside, a fire pit and a firebox made of clay showed signs of recent use.

"Someone's coming," Biku said. He pointed to a cleared swath through the standing grain. Rowan peered, and made out a tiny, stooped figure. Two of them, bent under heavy burdens.

At the hut, Embri and Linnit spilled bundles of grain from their backs. They both looked lean and fit. Linnit was burned darker than ever from the sun, and her arms and legs were wiry with new muscles. Both females greeted Rowan with pleased surprise.

He responded politely but guardedly. Embri was anxious to hear all the news of the village, and Rowan obliged her. While he talked, Linnit spread a hide to receive the seeds and began to beat the stalks into it. Biku helped her, and together they tossed the laden blanket to remove the chaff.

Their laughter annoyed Rowan. He broke off his narrative and turned to them. "Perhaps Biku should tell you the details of our trip," he said. "After all, he is supposed to be the trailmaker." He made his voice heavy with innuendo.

Both females focused on Biku as he shot Rowan a glance that was both angry and imploring.

Linnit held the blanket still. "Why, what happened?" she asked. "Did you run into shureks?"

Biku wet his lips. "We saw some at a distance," he said. "But they gave us no trouble. It was a safe trip, really—we had no problems at all." He began to shake his end of the blanket again vigorously.

Linnit matched his effort, smiling as the seeds danced and the chaff flew. Her eyes were bright.

Too bright, Rowan saw. They were almost feverish, with an aqueous overlay that he had learned to recognize as a sign that she would soon be into her rut.

Linnit seemed unconscious of any change in her physical condition. She emptied the blanket into a sack and started on a second bundle of grain. "How long can you stay?" She addressed both males. "We've more grain now than the four of us can carry, but there's so much out there"—she waved toward the fields—"that we can't make ourselves stop working."

"We wanted to leave a good supply here," Embri said. "Then, if we run out before the winter is over, someone might try a snow crossing."

They were both returning, then. Embri nodded at his unspoken question. "Yes, we've decided not to winter over. We'll be back next summer, though, for sure."

Rowan's stiff constraint began to loosen. Both Embri and Linnit were so relaxed and happy with their success that he felt foolish harboring a grudge. He smiled. "You've enjoyed it here? No, don't answer, I can see. But tell me: haven't either of you missed the ocean?"

"Linnit hasn't. Me—I've had some bad moments." Embri made a wry face. "More than I expected, but I got used to it." She dismissed the subject with a shrug. "What do you think of the house? Rintu wondered once what we could use for building materials. How surprised he would be—all we had to do was dig."

Linnit and Biku had finished another winnowing and were wandering off toward the stream. Rowan could hear her voice, high and excited.

Embri followed his gaze. "They're going to bathe. Messy business, getting out the seeds. Why don't you go, too, and I'll get started on a meal for all of us."

Rowan needed no urging. By the time he caught up with

them, Linnit had already peeled off her body wrap and Biku was shucking off his outer clothing. She was half a head taller than he, and so much narrower that they made a grotesquely mismatched pair. Watching them together, Rowan felt anger build in him like a slow fire. "Wait!" he shouted. He had to get Linnit away from Biku before her scent arose.

Linnit turned. She was not yet swollen, he saw, but there was suspicious moistness on the inside of her thighs.

She noticed it as he did. Her eyes widened and she ran like a frightend grauf over the stubbly field.

She was in the water when Rowan and Biku arrived at the bank. "A fine female," Biku said.

There must have been a scent, Rowan thought. He glared at Biku. How he hated him!

Biku persisted. "Didn't you say that the two of you aren't together anymore?"

Rowan tensed the muscles of his arms. He put his hands behind him and made fists. "I said no such thing. I don't recall discussing it at all."

"But everyone says she left you."

"Then they know more than I do."

"I say she's free." Biku spread his legs in a fighter's stance. He was stripped down to his loin wrap, his skin glistening with fine beads of sweat.

Rowan felt himself burning, too. He tore off his tunic and circled his rival, growling as he threw feinting blows.

Biku crouched and sprang. As they struggled on the mud-slick grass, Rowan was lost in the red haze of his pounding blood. He fought wildly, until Biku's weight pinned him flat and he couldn't move.

Rowan drew strength from desperation. Finally, he was able to break the holds. When they rolled into the water, he was on top. He forced Biku under and held him until the hand came up that signaled surrender.

Biku picked up his clothes and left as soon as he regained his breath. Rowan rested against the bank. The red haze went away, leaving him with nothing but a terrible desire.

Linnit waited in the middle of the stream. When Rowan

waded out to her, she moved back. "I'm sorry it happened," she said. "I should have noticed and kept away from Biku." Her eyes were glassy.

"You wouldn't have kept away from me?"

She turned and swam to the opposite bank, looking back to see if he was following.

Linnit lay quietly in his arms. They had made a soft, grassy bed and come together with the ease of familiarity. She was quickly sated, and as her musk faded, so was he. The sun warmed them to drowsiness until a swarm of insects descended, sending them slapping and screeching in a mad dash to the water.

"What if Biku had won?" Rowan asked when they were dressed again and on their way back to the hut.

"I don't know. I don't even want to think about it." Linnit wrinkled her face in a grimace of distaste. "I did wrong to let him catch my scent, so I suppose . . ."

She caught Rowan's hand. "But I knew you would win—I was never even worried. It's why I chose you, remember?"

"Surely not because I'm such a fighter. Any number in the tribe could down me."

She gave his fingers an impatient tug. "You know what I mean. That if I ever made a mistake like that one with Biku, you would save me from it. So there really wasn't any question of what I would have done."

She had gotten out of it cleverly. What would she think if she knew about him and Nithrin? he wondered. He had an uneasy suspicion that she wouldn't be as glibly tolerant of landling nature if the mistake applied to him.

However, she would probably never know. Linnit chattered on about her summer's adventures as naturally as if she and Rowan had never been separated. Maybe, he thought, it would not be so difficult after all.

When they reached the hut, Embri and Biku were sitting outside, eating. "Join us," Embri invited.

They did so, sitting and leaning comfortably against a sod

wall. "There's no meat," Embri apologized. "We haven't taken the time lately to hunt. But try this." She passed a bowl that contained flat, brown rounds of something warm and fragrant. "Linnit learned to make these, playing with her firebox."

Linnit grinned. "I thought: why can't I use it for cooking, too?" She pressed one of the rounds on Rowan, breaking it and holding it to his mouth. "We had all this grain and not much else, so I tried baking some of the mash." She giggled. "At first everything burned, but when I started using just a few hot coals . . ." She watched him eagerly while he tasted.

He smiled his approval.

Biku belched and reached for another. "This is even better than seagreens, and I never thought I'd hear myself saying that." He studied the firebox and turned to Linnit. "I'd like one for myself. Would you help me make it?"

"Of course. You and anyone else who wants one."

"You'll be busy," Embri said. She passed another bowl, which contained fresh, ripe muscales. "These grow by the stream farther down. We've picked a lot of them, and even dried some."

Rowan peeled off the spiny skin and sucked. Juice dribbled down his chin.

"What do you think of an established summer settlement here?" Embri asked. "A dozen or so from the tribe. Anyone except females who might be growing eggs."

"Even for them," Linnit said, "it wouldn't be such a hardship. They could always make it back to the ocean— that mountain crossing isn't so bad."

Biku disagreed. "We've been lucky so far. The Sonsi won't even try it."

"Them!" Linnit curled her lip. "Fish-eaters! They may not want to come here, but they take our grain fast enough."

"I like the idea of a settlement," Rowan said. "There should be lots of volunteers after they hear what you two have to say."

"The younger ones, anyway," Embri said.

Linnit gave her a narrow-eyed glance that set Rowan to wondering just how serious Embri's "bad moments" had been.

Embri answered them both. "I said I'd come back, didn't I? But you can't judge others my age by me. I've always been different—even from my landing. You know that I never had a proper waterlife."

Biku got up suddenly. "I've got to piss," he said. He disappeared behind the hut, and a few minutes later Rowan saw him walking toward the river.

"He doesn't want to hear anything about waterlives," Rowan said. "For some reason, it bothers him."

"That sounds familiar." Embri passed a water bowl for washing. "When I landed nobody would talk about it, either. Maybe we haven't changed so much, for all our new ways."

Rowan thought of the rage he had felt when he and Biku fought, and he had to agree with Embri.

Linnit objected. "Of course we've changed," she said. "I wouldn't be here otherwise. Or you either, Rowan." She ran a wet hand through the scales of her crest, pushing them into disarray. "Now, about those fireboxes . . ."

Under Linnit's direction, the conversation shifted to the merits of clay over stone. When the subject of fireboxes was exhausted, the three began to plan their departure from the valley. Another day would give Rowan and Biku a chance to rest, they decided. It would also enable the females to finish harvesting a particularly fruitful patch of grain.

Biku returned, and they settled down for an early night. The next day Rowan felt restored enough to join in the grain cutting. After a late waking, so did Biku. They added another half sack to the stores, and when they organized their gear for the return trip, each carried two full bags of grain.

Heavily burdened as they were, the journey back was slow and tedious. They took care to avoid any suspicious trails, and once more they were lucky.

The village was as Rowan had left it. Targ and his hunters had killed two shureks, but others continued to infest the outer forest. Foraging was poor, confined to a close area.

Rowan greeted friends on all the trails. He decided to store the grain at Embri's, and when he and Linnit came out of the hollow he was faced with more welcomers.

Linnit grew impatient and went on ahead. When at last Rowan came to his own clearing, he was surprised to see her running from the house.

She pushed away his hand. "Go in and see," she hissed.

Nithrin was waiting inside.

7

The air was thick with the scent of musk, driving everything else from Rowan's mind. Much later, when he could think again, he asked Nithrin what Linnit had said.

"Linnit?" Nithrin looked up from tying on her tunic. "You mean she was here?"

"Yes, just before I came in. But I don't suppose you noticed."

She shook her head. "You know how I am at these times."

Rowan sighed. It equaled the worst of his imaginings.

"I didn't know she was back," Nithrin said. "I heard you were and hurried over here—I didn't think you would mind. I certainly won't come again." She draped a cloak over her smoothly-sloping shoulders.

"No—wait." He couldn't lose her, too. "I don't know what will happen with Linnit. For now, it's too late to worry. Stay for a while and talk."

"Well..." She slipped off the cloak. "I did have something to ask you, about Arak." She settled herself again on the floor, folding her legs as sinuously as if she had no bones at all.

"How is he?" Rowan asked.

"That's what I'm concerned about. You know he's been working with Suri and Chula. They say he'll be a fine healer."

Rowan nodded. "I'm happy to hear that."

"It's all very well, but he still feels shamed. If he is ever to be headman, he has to wipe out the stain of being thought a coward. He has to prove himself, and by more than learning about herbs and poultices."

"You must have patience. I said it will be a long time before I give up the cape." Rowan had a disquieting thought. "Or did you see my death in that last vision of yours?"

"No, it was nothing like that." Nithrin plucked at the cloak folded on her lap. "I don't like to talk about my far-sights, because sometimes it brings bad luck." She braced herself visibly, and met his gaze. "But this—it was a good vision. I saw Arak, much older, wearing the cape."

"So why are you worried?"

"They don't always happen the way I see them. This one—I want to make sure it does."

"I don't see what you can do. Or me, either. Arak is taking the right course by learning a respected trade. The other—the tribe will forget."

She shook her head. "No, there is already a song. I heard Orkas's egg-issue singing it the other day, and some of the younglings took it up: 'Arak, Arak, how he ran.' And much more like that."

"Has he heard it?"

"Yes, and he agrees that there is only one way for him to recover his standing in the tribe. He has to bring in the head of a shurek."

Something cold twisted in Rowan's stomach. "Does he know what that means? Even the best hunters . . ."

"He knows. And he also knows that he has to go out secretly. I offered to go with him—I killed a shurek once, with the farsight to guide me—remember? But Arak won't have my help."

"So you want me to go?"

"He is your issue."

She waited, but Rowan could not give her the answer she wanted. Lost in confusion, he could say nothing.

It was foolhardy, what she asked. His own hunting skills were minimal, and Arak—who could tell about him? It was insane to even consider it.

Yet if what Nithrin said was true, Arak had no choice. Dishonored so young . . .

"You'll think about it, at least?" Nithrin rose to leave. "And you'll talk to Arak?"

Rowan assented.

Alone in the hut, he could think of nothing else. He thought of his easy assurances that the tribe would forget Arak's first failures. They wouldn't; he admitted it now. He thought of Biku and of how he himself had disparaged him as a failed trailmaker. He thought of Arak, so full of promise.

As he paced and muttered to himself, he found himself wishing that Issa had never told him of Arak's kinship. He would still be with Linnit, and Nithrin and Arak would be nothing to him. And why had he forced the admission from Nithrin? Now she expected him to risk his life for someone he barely knew.

Unworthy thoughts. Shaming thoughts that his better nature renounced. He might expect them from an old one like Mim, he reproved himself, but not from a headman of the new breed. No, he would never be sorry he had sired a line. But he was no longer a fool where Nithrin was concerned. He didn't trust her or the version she had told him of her vision. It presaged something ill for him, he was sure of it. Nithrin cared only about Arak; he had no illusions there.

He decided nothing, except that he would have to see Arak. Perhaps then he would know what to do.

He left at once, but Arak was not at home. He traced him to Suri's, where he came to the door at Rowan's call.

Linnit was inside as well. She squatted beside a grossly changed Suri, who was reclining on the bed. "I don't want to see you," Linnit said in an icy voice, showing Rowan only the back of her head.

Rowan motioned to Arak, and they stepped outside.

Arak looked thinner and older, with the softness gone from his face. He waited impassively, his eyes downcast, for Rowan to speak.

"I saw Nithrin, and she says you're doing well here. Has Suri taught you all she knows?"

He shrugged. "That you will have to ask her."

"But I'm asking you: are you ready to assume the trade?"

The face remained still. "If anyone will come to me. Which I doubt."

"I'm trying to help you, Arak," Rowan said with some heat. "Won't you at least look at me?"

Arak did, with brown eyes that were dull and cold. "How can you help me, headman? And why should you want to?"

"Because . . . because I am your egg-sire."

Rowan had not meant to say it, but the words were out and between them, hanging charged in the air.

A dark flush rose from Arak's neck ridges. It purpled his face. "Is this true? I don't . . . If it is, why haven't I known before?"

"I only found out myself not long ago." Rowan held out his hand. "It gave me much happiness. And pride."

Arak hesitated a moment before he crossed the hand with his. "The pride is all mine." He withdrew from the touch and averted his eyes. "You can feel nothing but shame."

"Come, walk with me a ways," Rowan invited. He waited, and Arak joined him. "You know of Marek, the headman before Roko."

"Of course. Nithrin talks about him all the time."

"Marek was dishonored, too, in the eyes of the tribe. He almost killed someone in a mating fight. Yet when Lors swam out without passing on the cloak, Marek won it easily and no one objected. Your . . . disgrace . . . is certainly no greater than the one he overcame."

"But it is!" Arak was a youngling again, perilously close to tears. "What I did—what they say I did—marks me as a coward. Marek was never that. He was chief hunter, and I . . . I . . . You know what I am."

Rowan spoke quietly. "Are you a coward, Arak?"

"No! I don't know why I threw so badly at the tusker, but it wasn't because I was afraid. I don't expect you to believe me, though. No one does."

"I believe you. I've seen it happen to others. Was the tusker charging?"

"No, it was just standing there. Then Alloran shouted at me and I had to throw. He says I almost hit him."

"Didn't you?"

"Maybe. I don't know. Targ believes him, and that's all that matters."

They walked for a while in silence. "Nithrin told me something else," Rowan finally said. "About your plan to go after a shurek."

Arak's mouth tightened. "She talks too much."

"You know that any hunting is forbidden for you. Targ hasn't relented."

"Of course I know! And I don't even have a spear—Targ saw to that. How would I kill one—with my hands?" He spread his fingers in a gesture of helplessness. "And now—I must get back to Suri."

"It's all right; Linnit is there."

"No, I promised. She wants to tell me about using ketter bark for fevers. She hasn't much more time." He made the sign of parting, but delayed his steps. "Do others know—about us?"

"Not yet."

Arak looked relieved. "Can it stay hidden for a while longer?"

"As long as you say. But why?"

"You'll know when the time comes. And I owe you thanks for telling me." He repeated the sign and ran back along the trail.

Rowan looked after him, deeply worried. He no longer

had doubts about wanting to help Arak; it was now a question of how he could do it. He thought: Nithrin would know when the youth planned to go. Probably she had obtained the spear he would use. He knew that Arak would not allow him to come along, but if he could follow secretly, perhaps he could do something to avert a tragedy.

Nithrin agreed, and promised to alert him before Arak left. She came the next morning with the message.

"He's going late today, with the last light," she said.

"Are you both mad?" Rowan clamped the muscles of his jaw. The most dangerous time! "If he's out there after dark. . . ."

"It's the only time he can go without notice. Targ has scouts on the trails all through the day."

"Is he coming to you first for the spear?"

"No, I've hidden it in the dead gourd tree at the beginning of the three-trees trail. I'll show you."

"I know where it is."

"Then you'll be there?"

"Didn't I say so?" He glared at her, and she stared just as furiously back. Both of us too frightened to trust one another, he thought.

Nithrin set her jaw, too. "If you let anything happen to him—"

"You'll what? Kill me with those soft hands?"

"Rest assured, I can do it."

"What about yourself?" he countered. "If it turns out badly, you'll be the one to blame. You encouraged him in this mad scheme."

Blotches flared in her cheeks. "I'll go myself, then, I *was* mad to come to you. I can protect him better than you. Better than anyone."

Rowan damped the hot words on his own tongue. It was no time for quarreling. "I'll do what I promised," he said. "I'll watch, and be ready with my spear if he needs help."

"But leave him the kill."

"If we both still live."

* * *

Rowan hid beside the trail until Arak came for the spear in the hollow tree. Targ's scouts had all gone home, and the young male hurried with no special caution into the dense outer forest.

Rowan followed, not too close but keeping him in sight.

Arak appeared to know exactly where he was going: he set a straight course into a stand of ancient, twisted gourds. Several of the massive giants had fallen, their rotted shells providing the kind of dark, soft lairs favored by shureks.

Rowan stayed well back and watched.

Arak made no attempt to conceal his presence. He tramped the area repeatedly, then took his position in the fork of a well-positioned tree. He had clear views all around and no obstructions.

Rowan found a perch in a gourd at the edge of the stand —well away, he hoped, from the scent Arak had spread. If a shurek should come to him instead. . . . He balanced his hunting spear and felt at his belt for the handles of his two throwing knives.

So far, all seemed well. They would have an hour of light, Rowan guessed. They might be lucky, if only an un-paired shurek appeared and if it appeared soon.

The evening fog betrayed them. It came thick and fast from the ocean, wrapping the forest in a gray shroud that was worse than darkness.

Rowan could barely see his own hands, let alone Arak. He cursed to himself and began to slide down the tree. Through the wall of mist he heard a cry, then a thudding, gasping noise. Something crashed through the underbrush with a great roar, and all around him was the suffocating, fetid odor of shurek.

"Arak, where are you?" Rowan shouted. He crouched, peering in all directions and seeing nothing. He held his spear ready, but the huge creature was on him before he could throw it.

Pain raked his face and his throwing arm. He was

knocked to the ground, the collapsed weight of the shurek on top of him.

He blacked out. How long, he didn't know. Finally something tugged at the crushing weight, moving it so he could breathe. Arak's face swam out of the mist. Rowan could see dimly with one eye; the other was a red, burning agony.

"The fever's gone. He should rest better now." The voice was Chula's, but the touch of soft lips on his brow signaled someone else. Rowan opened his good eye to see Linnit bending over him.

"He's awake," she called excitedly.

Chula's face joined Linnit's. "How do you feel?"

He tried to sit up, but the pain in his head forced him back. He remembered. "My eye. . . ."

"Don't touch it!" Chula cried. "And don't move the poultice. I don't want to have to tie your hands."

He lay still. "Just tell me: is it gone?"

"Yes, but the wound will heal. The ones on your arm, too."

His right arm, he saw, was heavily dressed. It felt numb. "Arak?" he asked.

Linnit answered, "He's fine. He brought you out, but he won't say anything about what happened. Targ found the shurek's body. Is it your head?"

"No, it's Arak's."

"But what were you doing off the trails so late?"

He grimaced painfully. "A fool's errand. I went to rescue someone who didn't need it. It seems I'm the one who did."

When word spread that Rowan was better, he had a stream of visitors. Arak came, grave and quiet in his new pride. Dak and Vani and Nimo, back from the Sonsis, came together. Nimo told of a successful sea voyage, and Dak of good trading. Vani was egg-swollen and happy. Cuma came, and reported a fair harvest of mussels. Issa told about a thriving hatchling house.

Nithrin did not come, nor did Rowan expect her to.

When Embri came, she was full of harsh words about both Arak and Nithrin. "When will she have done with our kin? They could have killed you, that poisonous flower and her cub."

Rowan checked to see that Linnit was listening. "He is my issue, too," he said.

Embri gasped. She looked at Linnit and away again quickly. Then she hurried out.

Linnit sat with folded hands. "You should have told me before."

"Does it make a difference?"

"Yes. I understand you now."

He thought, if only he could understand himself.

Part V

THE OLD ONES

1

It was black as a winter midnight when Embri left her bed. She stumbled over her water jar and muttered a curse; she was becoming clumsier every day.

There was no time to mop up the spill, even if she could have seen to do so. She hurried outside, anxious to search the sky before it was too late.

Biku had been the first to see Smallsun. Up early to prepare the soil in the long field for planting, he had reported two sunrises. Then Chula and Issa, on an all-night watch at the birthpools, had confirmed the phenomenon.

At first Embri hadn't believed it. During the day, with Bigsun lighting the sky, there was no noticeable difference. But now she too saw it: a red glow that appeared over the tallest stand of gourds slightly before Bigsun rose as usual out of the inner forest.

Embri stared at the spot, transfixed, until it was eclipsed by the brightness of the greater orb. But it was there, no mistake.

She looked away and rubbed at her temples. Even with

the sky normal again, she could not think coherently. There was so much to consider. Smallsun again, after all this time! After forty cycles, her entire landlife. After all of them learning new lives.

She had to tell Rowan. As she climbed up to the main trail, Embri moved stiffly. Her legs were heavy with the layer of fat that distended and dimpled her thickening skin. Her best gait was an Issa-like waddle on splayed feet that no longer flexed as they should for walking.

She looked down at the exposed portions of her limbs with distaste that bordered on revulsion. She, who had always been so thin! She wore a long, smothering mantle and heavy footwraps, in spite of the season, as much for her own vanity as to protect the sensibilities of others. As she sweated under the Sonsi cloth, she berated herself for foolishness. She had better get used to her new body; her change was still in the early stages. Nithrin, she understood, no longer showed herself at all.

Rowan and Linnit were breakfasting on grain cakes and greens when Embri burst in on them without waiting for permission. "It's true," she said with a quick sign of apology. "Smallsun is back."

Rowan frowned, grunted and continued to eat. The portions of his face not hidden by the eyepatch showed no reaction to the news.

Linnit rose to fetch another bowl. "Join us," she invited. "I cooked plenty."

"Didn't you hear me?" Embri repeated. She wasn't sure what response she had expected. Amazement, certainly. Perhaps joy or even fear. But certainly not indifference.

Rowan laid down his scoop. "More changes," he said. Deep, tired lines ringed his mouth. The last winter had been mild, with more rain than snow, but marauding shureks had driven off most of the game and the tribe was short of meat. Now the spring hatchlings in all the pools were ailing, and Embri knew that Rowan had been almost ill himself with worry. "So the others were right," he said. "I've had too much else on my mind to think about what was happening in the sky. You know best what it means. Tell me."

Embri was distracted by the steaming bowl of seagreens that Linnit set before her. They were cooked exactly right— just enough to release the juices but yet retain the texture. The aroma filled Embri's mouth with so much moisture that she could not speak. With an embarrassed glance at Rowan, she set to eating. When the bowl was half empty, she broke two grain cakes over the remaining greens and mixed them together. She scraped the sides of the bowl with a third cake, and only when she had swallowed the last crumb did she look up.

"I can make more," Linnit offered.

Embri shook her head in refusal, though she could easily have eaten another bowlful. Her appetite was insatiable, and though in private she gorged, here her pride restrained her.

Rowan put aside his own empty bowl. "So what does this return of the Smallsun mean to us?" he asked again. "What do you remember of the old time?"

"Nothing," Embri said. "It was nearly over when I landed. But everyone talked about it. They said that the forest used to be full of food and no one was ever cold or hungry. It seems they lived without a care."

"Do you believe it?"

Embri shrugged. "Rintu said it, too, and why would he lie?"

Linnit squatted beside Rowan and placed her hand on his shoulder. "Suri used to tell us about the long-days, when it was never dark."

"Yes, it sounds wonderful, doesn't it?" Rowan's bitter tone mocked his words. "Can you tell me, then, why the hatchlings are dying?"

"Still?" Embri forgot about the sky and what it signified.

"Two more yesterday," Rowan said. "One was Kalina's. None of the hatchlings are losing their waterskins, though they're well past the size. Kalina took hers out of the pool anyway, it was so ill, but of course she couldn't make it breathe."

"Nithrin won't come to look inside them," Linnit said. "And Issa doesn't know what to do."

"Can't you talk to Nithrin?" Embri said to Rowan. She couldn't resist a shaft. "There was a time—or is it possible she can have forgotten you?"

"She won't see me."

She gave up the teasing. "Maybe Arak—"

"Or him, either."

Embri shifted her weight. She could no longer squat, and the floor, even with the hides, pressed hard against her buttocks. Her legs ached and there was no way she could arrange them comfortably. If only she could stretch out. . . .

Both Linnit and Rowan stared at her expectantly. Embri knew what they waited for her to say. Ah well, she thought, at least she could still be of some use. "Why do you think Nithrin would see *me*?" she asked. "You know how it has always been between us."

"Because of your...condition," Rowan said. "She wouldn't feel ashamed, with you, of how she looks. If you could persuade her to come to the pools, to tell us what it is that's wrong with the hatchlings. . . ."

"I'll try," Embri promised. "But if she's as far along as I imagine, she won't be able to walk that distance." She thought a moment. "Has Kalina taken her dead one to the beach yet?"

"Yes, Chula and I went with her last night," Linnit said. "We sent it off with a fine deathsong." She cleared the bowls and scoops from the hearth, putting them aside for washing. "I wish I hadn't gone, though." Her voice was strained. "It was all too familiar."

Rowan glanced at her with an anxious frown, but Linnit appeared absorbed in studying the glazing on her water pitcher. He turned back to Embri. "We could carry Nithrin, if she'll agree to go."

"She won't, if it means being seen. I was thinking, instead, of taking one of the hatchlings to her. One that had recently died."

Rowan's good eye registered shocked surprise. Embri

prepared to defend her suggestion, but after a short silence he nodded. "Well, why not? I'll go out to the pools and see what has happened during the night. The chances are there'll be one for you there now."

"No, I'll go," Embri said. She hauled herself awkwardly to her feet. "I should walk more, to keep from getting so stiff." She looked up at Rowan, who had risen, too. "You wanted to know about Smallsun, and I couldn't give you any answers. I still can't, except one: I don't have to tell you, do I, what it means to me?"

Rowan stared, and Embri did not explain further. Outside, she forgave him for not immediately grasping her meaning. He had enough worries without speculating about something so common as the final transformation of an aging female, even one who happened to be his egg-source. She couldn't blame him when she had wanted it that way, purposely making light of her change. She had hidden from him as well as from Issa and Dak the shortness of breath that troubled her, the constant hunger and the aching joints. So why should Rowan think of her now in a personal connection with Smallsun? As headman, he was concerned with the ailing new life, and rightly so. Soon enough he would see the pattern in all of it, but she would not be the one to tell him.

Let the other one do it, she thought as the old grudge returned. Let Nithrin, with her precious inner sight, reveal the unwelcome news. Embri knew what Nithrin would see when she looked into the dead hatchlings, but let her be the one to announce it to the tribe.

As she approached the edge of the forest, Embri stopped to catch her breath. It came raspingly, in short, panting gasps. Lately she felt a constant pressure in her chest, and when she exerted herself it was worse.

Her legs, too, protested their punishment. The knifelike pains that shot up with each step subsided to a dull throbbing as she rested, and her poor, abused flipper-feet were numb as blocks of wood.

She wouldn't have attempted the walk just for Rowan.

She had a more compelling reason for punishing herself than the one she had given him: the birthpools beckoned like oases of relief. If Issa was there alone, she could submerge herself completely and ease every pressure of her tortured flesh.

She thought of water constantly, and lately she had begun to dream of it. When a breeze brought her a whiff of the sea, she found the strength to continue her journey. On the dunes, looking toward the ocean, she felt both a yearning and an aching sadness. Behind her the forest spread sheltering arms, and it seemed to her that she could never bear to give up what she had known there. Would her mindset finally change, too, she wondered, releasing her from all land ties? Rintu, she remembered, had begged to be freed though he had known it meant his death.

For her, there was now another possibility. Cuma, the last to go into the ocean, had lived there for two hands of days before her body had been found, and that had been in midwinter. If Smallsun continued to grow stronger. . . . Embri searched the sky where it should be showing, and she fancied that she could make out a faint white glow.

She mustn't speculate too much, she warned herself. Not when she was about to view other consequences that weren't a cause for hope.

The tide was out, and she picked her way over sand and rocks to the natural basin of the big birthpool. As Rowan had predicted, a dead hatchling lay outside. It was over two hands in length, but when Embri turned it over she found that its waterskin was still perfectly intact.

The remaining smaller hatchlings swam sluggishly through strands of rotting seagreens. Issa, on her stomach at the rim of the pool, was attempting to remove the slimy tentacles with a netted pole. She saw Embri and sat up. "They won't take their food," she said. "I don't think these old greens really hurt them—they never have before—but I don't know what else to do."

"Let me help you," Embri said. She removed her footwraps and robe and eased herself into the water. Issa handed her the net, and Embri held it out before her as she glided back and forth across the pool.

She moved as sleekly as a swimmer, with no more effort than a flip of her feet and a twist of her body. While Issa cleaned the green-clogged webbing, she played like a swimmer, too, luxuriating in her lightness and mobility.

She almost forgot who she was. When she came up chuffing and sputtering from a shallow dive, the tightness in her chest reminded her that she was only half changed.

Issa leaned over the rocks and reached down a stubby arm. "Are you all right? Here, let me help you out."

Embri floated away. "No, I'll stay awhile longer. I feel better in here as long as I remember that I don't have water-slits yet."

"But aren't you cold?" Issa tugged her wrap around her shoulders.

"Not at all." Embri no longer hated her blubbery layer of insulation. She wondered, though, if it was the only reason she wasn't freezing. Surely the hatchlings, too, perceived a change. "Don't you think the pool is warmer?" she called up.

Issa tested the water with a foot. "Not that I can notice." Her face wrinkled in a thoughtful frown. "Are you sure?"

Embri nodded.

"Do you suppose the hatchlings feel it?"

"They might. At least it's something to consider. I saw Smallsun, too, this morning."

Issa gazed woefully into the pool, then beyond it to the empty smaller ones. "I've heard all my life, if the other sun ever came back, it would be something wonderful. An end to all our bad times." She snorted. "Some gift it brings us!"

"There'll be more eggs laid," Embri said. "It's too early yet to say what will become of all of them."

"But you can guess, can't you?" Issa continued gloomily.

"Don't think about it now," Embri said. "Give me that net, and I'll finish cleaning the pool. Then I'll take the dead hatchling to Nithrin. Maybe she can tell us exactly why it died."

Issa said no more, but Embri suspected that they shared the same forebodings. Embri finished her task and climbed out of the pool. Just as she finished dressing, Chula and Mogian came to relieve Issa. When they learned where Embri was going, they insisted on coming along.

Issa objected. "Someone has to stay here," she said. "And not me. I've been on watch all night, and I'm tired."

"I'll come back," Chula promised. "After I've heard what Nithrin has to say. As a healer—"

Mogian cut her off. "It's more important for me to go." She patted her swollen stomach. "I have to know what to expect."

They all looked at Embri. "Issa and Chula can come with me," she decided. "Mogian, you'll hear soon enough if we learn anything. Actually, I don't know if Nithrin will admit any of us. Rowan thinks I should try to see her alone."

Mogian grumbled, but settled down to watch the pool. The others set off, and with Chula and Issa to lean on, Embri made the journey back to the forest without too much discomfort.

"I'll leave you two here," Issa said when they came to Nithrin's grove. "I wouldn't be any help getting you in to see her, and I'm about to fall asleep on my feet."

"I thought . . . won't Nithrin even admit *you*?" Embri had counted on Issa's influence.

"Not for three hands now." The words were harshly abrupt.

"How does she get food?"

"She has stores inside. I leave seawater and fresh greens at her door, and so does Arak. She doesn't eat much anymore." Issa handed Embri the seaweed-wrapped corpse. "If you do get to talk to Nithrin, give her a message." She stood close, but murmured so softly that Embri had to strain to hear. "Tell her that I'll always see her as the red flower. She shouldn't shut me out now." She turned her head, and Embri could see her shoulders shaking.

Would you grieve as much for me? Embri wondered. She

tried to dismiss the pang of jealousy, but it persisted. It would be a contest to the end, she thought.

Issa left, and Embri and Chula crossed the clearing. Embri signaled to Chula to stand aside while she announced herself at the door.

A surprisingly strong voice answered the second call.

2

"You can leave that dead thing outside and come in, both of you." A long, rasping cough followed the words.

Embri put her bundle down, and with Chula behind her, she entered Nithrin's house for the first time.

It was dankly cold, for all the wealth of furs on the walls. Nithrin rested on a bed of soggy moss, covered, except for her head, by a wet graufskin blanket.

She could have been any old one: sexless without her crest, her features all but lost in the swollen lumpiness of her face. "Stare! Stare all you want," she croaked. "It'll happen to you, too, Chula. And you, Embri—it won't be long for you now."

Embri repressed a shudder. It wasn't Nithrin's words that affected her, or her appearance, but the unbearable contrast as the other Nithrin, still young and lovely, looked out of the gross creature's eyes.

She had felt it in herself. Her old form, her true form, trapped in the changing body. She regarded Nithrin with a sympathy she hadn't anticipated. "Yes, we two are the last from our landing," she said. "I thought, once, that we might be going back together."

Nithrin's other self vanished in a spasm of wheezing. "I can't wait. I'm ready now." The huge body heaved under the blanket.

Embri winced as she felt the pain in her own flesh. "Do you want us to help you to the ocean?" she asked.

"Yes, but not until dark." Nithrin's every breath seemed to be drawn with an agonizing effort. "Get Issa, too. Can you three do it?"

Chula came forward. "We can manage. But will you do something for us first?"

Nithrin motioned for them to come closer. "I know what you want," she said in a whisper. "And you don't need me. Cut the hatchling open, and you'll see that its air-breathers aren't ready. All of them in that pool will die—Smallsun will see to it."

Chula gasped and started to protest, but Embri waved her to silence. "How do you know about Smallsun?" she asked.

"I've seen it. And what will happen."

"And have you seen yourself living in the ocean?"

Something—it could have been a smile—moved across Nithrin's face. She did not answer Embri, however, but focused on Chula. "Do you want to save the hatchlings?"

Chula nodded, her mouth tight and her eyes wide.

"Then open the birthpool."

"But—you know that they'll die in the ocean."

"Not any more."

Chula turned to Embri. "Do you believe it? How can that be?"

"It was the old way," Embri said.

"But . . . the little pools . . ."

"Death traps now," Nithrin whispered.

Chula sank to her haunches. As she stared from Embri to Nithrin, her mouth opened and closed soundlessly. When she finally found words, her voice was strangled. "But if we did that, if we opened the pool, we wouldn't know what happens to our eggs or our hatchlings. We wouldn't see them again."

"You'd see them when they landed," Embri said. "When they were grown."

"But we wouldn't know them! We wouldn't know which were ours. They'd be strangers." She shook her head. "Why, it would be worse than using the common birthpool. It's monstrous to even think of it."

Nithrin looked at Embri, and again a movement flitted across the swollen face. "You'll get used to it," she said.

No one spoke, and in the ensuing silence Embri heard something outside. Footsteps and the clinking of stacked pottery.

"Nithrin!" It was Arak's voice on the other side of the door.

Nithrin stiffened. "Shhh!" she whispered warningly.

"Just let me know that you're all right," the voice begged.

Nithrin drew a long, shuddering breath. "Go away," she said in a voice as steady as she could manage. "I'm fine. Just go away." The effort cost her a spasm of choking, but she held off the sounds until the footsteps departed.

Chula brought in the water jars and the bowls of fresh greens. Embri picked up a bowl and carried it to Nithrin. "Let me help you to eat," she offered. She had done it for Rintu, she remembered. A service of love.

"No, leave it," Nithrin whispered. She closed her eyes and appeared to sleep.

Embri joined Chula at the door. "Until tonight," she said to Nithrin, not expecting an answer.

"Don't tell anyone," came a feeble response. "Not Arak, even. Not . . . to see me like this." She drifted off again.

Embri and Chula left quietly. They looked for the dead hatchling outside, but it was gone. Chula made a sound of disgust and strode angrily across the clearing. When Embri caught up with her at the trail, she was still fuming. "Arak! He's taken it, and you can be sure he'll find exactly what

Nithrin told us. He probably heard her. Air-breathers! How does he even know what to look for?"

"Would you," Embri asked.

"No," Chula admitted. "But it makes no difference. I know Nithrin was lying. The hatchlings are dying from something else—some sickness that will run its course in time. We've had them before."

"Not this kind." Embri started to say more, but decided that Chula was in no frame of mind to hear reason. "Are you going to tell Mogian?" she asked.

"With her so near her eggtime? I wouldn't think of it!"

"Don't you think she should hear, at least, and decide for herself?"

Chula regarded Embri coldly. "You believe Nithrin, don't you?"

"I'm going to see what Arak says."

Chula snorted again. She gave Embri the most perfunctory of parting signs and took the trail back to the beach.

Embri followed a branching path that led to Arak's house. She considered going home first, but curiosity overruled her hunger and her aching legs. She had to know what Arak discovered about the hatchling. She had no doubts that Nithrin had described a true vision, but Chula's reaction convinced her that the tribe would need more solid proof.

She tried to imagine herself in Chula's position, still fertile and with three generations of known issue. She might feel as threatened, she allowed, if she had a landlife yet before her.

Chula would get over it, though. Rowan and Issa, she remembered, had as younglings been more precious to her than her place in the tribe. But when she had been exiled and had left Dak to be raised by others, she had survived her grief. Now it seemed to her that they were all bound more by friendship than by their shared physical kinship. Dak and Vani's offspring, indeed, were scarcely closer to her than any other landlings.

Not Arak, however. More than either Rowan or Dak, he put her in mind of Rintu. He had the same voice, the same eyes, the same quiet yet assured manner. He was adept at any calling in the village, and despite Nithrin's influence he did not hold himself above the least.

He would examine the hatchling fairly, Embri knew. Chula had let anger distort her thinking. Arak had not even seen Nithrin recently, according to Issa, so it was unlikely that he would have heard of her latest vision.

Embri stopped to rest frequently, and by the time she reached Arak's clearing he was leaving his house.

He carried something wrapped in leaves. "Is that the hatchling?" Embri asked.

Arak started. "It was you who left it for Nithrin?" Rintu's eyes chided her. "But why? She has troubles enough now, without being blamed for these deaths. I would think that you could put old feuds behind you."

"No, no, you misunderstood," Embri said. "No one blames Nithrin. Rowan thought she might be able to tell why the hatchling died."

Arak's face cleared. "Ah, I see. Then perhaps I can help. I opened the body, to find the same answer for myself.

"Curious, what I discovered. The landling bones were still soft, and the airsacs had barely started to form. For some reason, the hatchling didn't change when it should."

"Is that why it died?"

"I don't know. If it is, they'll probably all meet the same fate. Perhaps . . ." He squinted up at the sky. "You've heard about Smallsun?"

"Yes." She wanted to say more, but stopped herself. He would figure it out for himself.

Arak looked down at his bundle. "I'll give it proper ceremony. It was from the common birthpool, wasn't it?"

"Kalina's was the last from the others."

"Then I'll take it to the rocks. And—there's no need to disturb Nithrin, for any reason. You understand, don't you."

Did he think she would go there to taunt? Embri felt a rush of shaming heat that he should know her so little. Here again, she thought, Nithrin had won.

She plodded home. The forest was stirring to summer

life, leafy overhead and rank with viny growth beside the trails. Two morning foragers whom she met had found gray-caps in the deep shade, and they gave her a pouchful.

She would stew them with tubers, Embri thought. With a flavoring of dried meat. Her mouth filled with drool and her stomach became a rumbling, hollow cavern. She stumbled on, oblivious to everything but her hunger, until finally the trail descended and she crossed the stream into her own clearing.

Safely inside her house, she shrugged off the sweaty cloak and splashed herself with water. She stirred the fire and built it up, filled her deep cooking pot and hung it on the frame. When the tubers were boiling she threw in the gray-caps and the slivers of meat, then added a handful of grain.

She edged back from the heat. Nithrin, she had noticed, had one of the new fire pits that were built into the wall.

Useless, of course, now. Soon, Embri knew, there would be no fire for her either. When she leaned over the pot to stir, her drying skin felt as if it would crack.

She ate the stew half cooked, reclining against a spot of bare wall. At first the stone felt cool and smooth against her flesh, but soon it began to bruise her. She pulled the fur hanging back into place and resettled herself, stretching out nearly straight. She thought of the pool where she had swum with such ease, and of the boundless freedom of the ocean beyond it. When she fell asleep, she was there beneath the green waves.

She slept through most of the day. Once she heard Rowan calling, but she was half in her dream and unwilling to leave it. After a while, he went away. She woke briefly to eat again, cold mash and greens that were none too fresh, but they filled her enough that she could slip back into her cool watery world.

It was late afternoon when she finally roused herself. She struggled stiffly to her feet and set about making yet another meal. She knew that she should go to see Rowan—he would be waiting to hear what she had learned from Nithrin—but she couldn't summon the energy.

He would find out soon enough. Everyone would, and there would be as much consternation as when she and Rintu had entered the village nearly forty cycles ago with the first land hatchling.

It seemed longer ago than that, thinking back. She had been so young and determined. Afraid of nothing. Now, when she looked at herself she saw an aging lump who slept all day and scarcely gave a thought to the sick hatchlings in their prison. The old Embri would have torn down the wall and braved the wrath of the tribe. The half-creature that she was now thought only of her stomach.

A tear ran down her face and into her bowl. For all the promise of her waterdreams, she would give them up without a qualm if she could have the merest portion of her youth back. If only she could relive those early cycles with Rintu. She had been so impatient with him, so angry with everyone in the tribe. If only she could try it again with the knowledge and understanding she had now. She needn't have made so many enemies. And Rintu—if only she could tell him what she had never been able to say. Had he ever really known what he meant to her?"

If only's. She scolded herself: nothing but futility, to dwell on them. Maunderings. She wiped her face and forced herself back to the present. Chula and Issa would be calling for her soon, and she had another long walk ahead of her.

She wiped out her bowl and put it with the others. She hadn't washed any of them properly for days—who would know or care? She hadn't seen to her water jars, either. Fortunately, one was half filled; she needed it for her parched skin.

The sponge bath brought little relief. It was time for her to start using seawater, she knew, much as she hated to ask Dak or Rowan to keep her supplied. She dressed in a loose tunic and laid ready a short mantle. No need to cover up; darkness would hide the unsightliness of her legs.

She stretched out again to wait. Night filled the summer window, and no one came. Perhaps . . . yes, she thought, they would have gone to get Nithrin first. She decided to meet them at the main trail, to save someone the trip down into the hollow.

The early moon was up, showing its thin face. It gave grudging light, but enough that Embri needed no torch. She could have walked the path blind, she thought. There, looming ghostly to her left, was the pile of stones that Rintu had gathered for a smokehouse. After he had gone, she had never wanted it finished. To her right was the clump of frangis that they had decided not to clear. Stepping carefully as she descended to the stream, she circled the mounds of debris left by the winter floods. At the crossing place, the stones were white splotches in the dark water. She remembered how precisely Rinu had placed them, to the measure of her steps. She heard a splash and then she saw him, wet and naked, wading ankle-deep in the stream.

She called out to him, and as she did so the sound shattered his image.

She shook her head sharply. Weak-brained old female. She had smiled on such lapses in other old ones, but now, when she couldn't keep her own mind from slipping, there was nothing amusing about it.

Climbing uphill, she was safe from her dreams; it required all of her concentration just to keep moving. She had barely recovered her wind when Chula and Issa arrived, carrying Nithrin on a pole-bed.

Chula supported the front end easily, but Issa was humped under the weight of the rear poles. Embri relieved her of one, and they continued through the forest.

Nithrin was a huge dark mound on the carrier. Embri could hear her labored breath, which almost matched her own. They proceeded without conversation. Embri was straining too hard to attempt any, and Chula and Issa, if they had done so, had apparently been rebuffed.

Chula halted when they came out of the trees. She looked back at Nithrin. "Where shall we take you?" she asked.

Nithrin waved what had been her hand toward the landing beach. They struggled over the dunes and lowered the litter where the beach began to slope.

The three bearers stood quietly, resting. "You can go," Nithrin said in a harsh whisper.

Chula strode off down the beach, and Issa put her hands to her trembling mouth. Embri waited until she could breathe again, then inclined herself to Nithrin. "Is there . . . any message for anyone?"

Nithrin had already rolled off the litter. Her eyes gleamed in the darkness as she looked up, but it was Issa she addressed. "Send them," she wheezed.

Issa stopped her crying and leaned down, too. "What do you mean?"

"You know. Send them to me." Nithrin rolled again, onto her stomach. She humped her way into the water and a wave covered her. When it receded, she was gone.

3

"Are you listening to me?" Mogian's petulant voice pulled Embri from her reverie. She had been imagining herself back in the grain valley, digging out chunks of earth for another sod house. It had been the snug, cavelike dwelling from her second summer there, carved out of the bank where the bluff rose so high over the river. When it was finished, from the door opening one could look down to the lapping water, and on the roof, standing in the grass and flowers, you couldn't tell there was a house beneath you.

"Embri?" The green field faded, replaced by dark walls and Mogian's frown. It was two days after Nithrin's going, and Mogian had come to Embri with a worried, complaining monologue.

"Yes, I heard you," Embri said. She hadn't—only the first words—but she could guess the rest. "You were wondering about the little birthpools—if I thought they were safe to use."

Mogian nodded and patted her egg-mound. "I have to

decide soon. Since Issa opened the big pool, I haven't known what to think.

"Yes, I know why she did it; you don't have to tell me. Chula doesn't believe it, though. She says..." She began again her harangue against Issa and the departed Nithrin.

This time Embri heard her out. "I wonder, then, why no one has built the wall back," she observed when Mogian was finished. "At least, it was still open when I was there this morning."

"That doesn't mean anything," Mogian said. "No one is concerned about the hatchlings in that pool. Let them swim away. But those of us who want our own..." She looked at Embri reproachfully. "I thought you, more than anyone, would understand."

Embri did understand, but she couldn't tell Mogian what she wanted to hear. "Go ahead and use one of the little pools," she said, "if you don't mind losing a clutch of eggs. Try it and see."

"Of course I would mind." Mogian straightened with a jerk that rattled her crest. "Just because I had all those younglings with Nimo, it doesn't mean I don't care this time. The fact is, it's more important than ever for me to raise one." She lowered her voice. "If Alloran doesn't get a youngling of his own, I don't think he'll stay with me. It's why he chose me, I'm sure—because he knows I'm fertile."

"Nonsense," Embri said. "I can't believe it would make such a difference to him."

Mogian sighed. "You don't know Alloran."

"Then it would be no loss to you if he does leave." If Mogian had been concerned for her eggs rather than for herself, Embri might have offered her sympathy. As it was, she felt only irritation.

"I should have expected that from you." Mogian raked Embri with her glance. "What could you know, in your condition!" She left, stiff-backed with anger, and Embri couldn't bring herself to care. What did it matter now what anyone thought of her?

Once it had been different, she remembered. In the first

cycles of her landlife she had longed more than anything to
have friends in the village. But after she and Rintu had returned from exile and were finally accepted, she had not
been able to forget the earlier injuries. It was she who had
chosen the isolated hollow for their house, overcoming
Rintu's objections. She had thought they could have another
family there, at last free from interference. But there had
been no more younglings, and they had settled into a reclu-
sive life, the two of them depending wholly upon one another.

*She sat with Rintu inside the tight stone house, both of
them sewing by firelight. The wind moaned outside and the
snow swirled; too dangerous to even attempt to cross the
hollow. But they had wood piled against all the walls, inside
and out, and their storage hole did not show bottom. When
the storm subsided they would tramp the clearing on foot-
frames looking for snowgreb mounds, and in the forest they
would search for the rootwort diggers that lived there even
in the coldest part of the winter.*

*Rintu got up to stir the fire, and a spark fell on Embri's
foot. She reached to brush it off, but for some reason she
couldn't move properly.*

The pain brought her back to reality. She threw water on
her foot, where the thickening skin had dried and puckered,
closed her eyes and tried to return to the same scene.

She couldn't, though she continued to think about that
winter and all the others with Rintu. The seasons had passed
as quickly, it seemed to her now, as one day. She had been
content, and she had thought that Rintu was, too. But Mogian's visit set her off on a sea of troubling speculations.
Perhaps Mogian was right about Alloran. And perhaps he
wasn't unique. If Rintu had known that there would be no
more hatchlings to raise, if she had offered him a free
choice, what would he have done?

Others had stayed together as long as they had, she told
herself. Targ and Chula. Dak and Vani. Rowan and Linnit,
for all their problems. Many more from the newer generations.

They had all been land-raised, however. Rintu had not.

Why, then, had he stayed with her? She knew herself as she had always been: ugly, short-tempered, and with a clacking tongue. She had a knowledge of the woods, true, and it had saved them once, but back in the village that was no longer so important.

Had it been gratitude? Or simply habit? She hated both possibilities.

Her head began to throb. She splashed her face with sea-water and covered it with wet moss and stretched out on the floor. Why was she given to such fruitless conjectures? If she couldn't keep her mind from running on, it would be better to concern herself with real problems. With helping Rowan.

He needed her, but she couldn't tell him how to calm the villagers. Smallsun would fulfill its promise, and there was nothing they could do.

There was nothing she could do, either, but endure to the end.

She tried to find a relaxing position, but her gnawing stomach interfered. She got up and ate some cold grain mash that Linnit had left and sipped from the water pitcher.

The water was oily, with a metallic taste. She spat it out and drank from the jar of seawater instead.

Finally, she was able to return to the rest that Mogian had interrupted. She needed it badly; the benefits of her morning swim had been more than undone by the walk back. It would soon be too much for her, she knew, but how could she give up her one pleasure? She wondered if she could build a shelter for herself at the beach. If Smallsun continued to grow stronger, she might be able to live there until her trans-formation was complete.

Thinking of warm sunshine and waiting for sleep, she went back to the summer of the dugout. It had been a small, happy village there in the valley. Three hands of them, hunt-ing and building and exploring the mountains while the grain ripened. She and Linnit, honored as leaders. If only. . . .

Embri thrashed on the hard floor as the rest of it came back, too. If only *he* hadn't been there. The trailmaker, Prem.

She saw him watching her from across the fire. She sat well away from the others, wrapped so tightly that no scent could possibly escape. She was safe, she knew, if that was what she wanted.

The red glow burnished his muscular shoulders. He smiled, and she was no longer sure about anything.

She had been so positive that there would be no one after Rintu. It would be no problem, she had assured Linnit; she could control herself in her heats. She had been so self-confident, so smugly superior. It had been nothing to Prem, but to her it had been an overwhelming shame. Especially when she had proven fertile and workers had to leave the harvest to escort her over the mountains to the ocean.

Her eggs had gone into the common pool and the dugouts she designed had all been flooded the next winter. If she had deserved to be humbled, nothing could have been more fitting.

She had found herself no different from others, after all. She had tried to change landling nature, in her puffed-up pride. Now, she thought, with Smallsun back it would be as if she had never dug that first sandy pool.

Her head ached again, and she trickled more water onto the moss that covered her eyes. She remembered how she had done it for Rowan when he had been a hatchling. She had been frantic, wanting so desperately for him to live. She saw him as he had looked then, a scrawny creature with skin beginning to peel, belonging more to the sea than the land.

He leaped from her arms and swam out into the ocean, and with a cry she followed him. They sported together in the white-tipped waves, light and free as the froth itself.

Embri continued to change, until she was a prisoner in her house as she was in her body. Rowan had refused to help her with the beach shelter—she would not be safe, he said —but he built her a bed of springy boughs covered with moss that cradled her unwieldy frame. He put the winter stone into the window when the light began to hurt her eyes, and she lived in shadows. When she was awake it was the world of her past, each event relived in well-remembered detail, and when she slept she was already in her waterlife. She roused herself to try to focus on Rowan and Dak and Issa when they came to see her, but their chatter was like the squawking of seabirds. For all her concentration, she knew that her responses made little sense to them.

It was better when each one came alone. With only one voice to follow, she could manage a conversation, and out of gratitude for their concern she pretended an interest in matters that were no longer important to her.

Issa came the most often. She missed her hatchlings and she missed Nithrin, and she questioned Embri avidly about every symptom of her changing.

Embri knew what was in her mind. "It will come, Issa," she said in the wheezing whisper that she found easiest for speech. "You can't hasten it, and you shouldn't want to. We don't know yet that the ocean will be kind to any of us."

"But we do know," Issa refuted her. "Nithrin is still out there, and the hatchlings, too. Mogian's eggs all rotted, did I tell you? Now everyone is using the open pool.

"You'll be needed," she said with a sigh. "But me: what will I do when the last youngling leaves the long house?"

Issa's lugubrious face swam disembodied above Embri. Her poor, stunted issue, she thought. Never quite a landling. A pain that was not physical welled up from somewhere within her, and she raised herself up on her bed to ease it.

The face was closer now, and it was the same tearful one that she had left behind her that terrible time of her exile. A film covered Embri's eyes, and she was back in the clearing before the freestanding house, walking between hostile ranks of villagers while Issa's sobs echoed in her ears.

"Embri, what is it? What's the matter?" Hands gripped her and lowered her back to the bed. Coolness bathed her face. The film cleared and the keening sobs stopped as Embri fought for the breath that she had exhausted.

Issa hovered with water and wet moss. Embri lay still,

and the pain in her chest eased. "I didn't want to leave you that time," she whispered. "You know it now, don't you?"

"Whatever are you talking about?" Issa replied. "You mustn't excite yourself. Rest now, and I'll fix you some greens and mash. You're sure you don't want it warmed? I could make a fire outside."

Embri closed her eyes. "No. And no mash. Just greens and water." She had lost her taste for cooked foods. A very little sufficed to fill her now, though it seemed to her that she was huge beyond imagining.

Embri pretended to sleep. She heard Issa place the bowl by the bed, do some housekeeping chores and finally leave. Then she was free to take herself away, to the bare, treeless village of the Sonsi.

The sounds and the smells assaulted her, but overriding them was her intense excitement. She squeezed Rintu's hand and received an answering pressure as the huge, ornamented figure of the headman came to meet them.

They were pushed ahead of a crowd into the Sonsi house, she still clinging tightly to Rintu's hand, when everything around her began to waver. The squatting figures dissolved into ripples. Cool, soft, green-tinged. She swam for hours, a blissful eternity, until Rowan's voice dragged her to the surface.

Again, she fought the burning pain in her chest.

His voice came to her from a distance. "Issa said... Here, let me look...." She felt something at the tender, fleshy ring that had been her neck. "No, you're not ready yet, but you shouldn't be here alone. Linnit will stay with you from now on, or Issa or myself." He replaced the moss coverlet.

She forced herself to concentrate. "Linnit, then," she whispered. "You must have more important things to do." She added, for politeness, not really caring: "How does it go outside? With Smallsun, I mean?"

The face with the eyepatch stopped moving in and out of the shadows. It settled in a space near her own. "Do you really want to know? Can you understand me?"

She caught his urgency, and it spurred her to push aside the remaining mists. She was left exposed and hurting, but clearheaded. "Yes, to both," she said. She wriggled herself half upright to better maintain her attention.

Rowan arranged himself in a spraddled squat. "Smallsun grows brighter every day," he said. "Biku's podplants are knee high and his grain thicker than that in the meadow, but both are dying for lack of rain."

"Why not carry water?" Embri said. "We all did before."

"That was then," Rowan said. "Now, no one wants to sweat under heavy water jars. The forest promises to give enough food that such labor seems useless."

"Ah. You worry that the old times are returning."

"Yes. And that we will lose more than we gain."

Embri understood. Rowan feared what would happen to the new breed if life were too easy. Dreaming under a tree instead of working to improve their lot.

"What if we should forget this?" Rowan picked up a glazed bowl of Linnit's. "Or this." He seized a tally stick. "And would we need this"—he pointed to the door that opened on leather hinges—"and what about the grain valley? Will anyone go there again, or even remember it?" His agitation increased. "If Smallsun disappears once more, who will know how to raise the hatchlings?"

"We have the watersongs," Embri said.

"Are there really such things?"

She answered without hesitation, recognizing her journeyings into the past for what they were. "I am sure of it. I feel them in me all my dreaming hours. I see them as clearly as I see you, and when I go, I will take them with me."

"Perhaps. But if you are wrong. . . ."

"Then we'll be as we were when I landed. But I don't think that can happen if other old ones are like me."

Rowan still frowned, but Embri could do no more to convince him. She sank back on her bed, exhausted by her effort. She motioned for the water jar, wet her mouth and managed a further whisper. "You will be the next to go, Rowan. So your answers are in yourself."

Rowan watched with a helpless, frightened look while Embri struggled for breath. "You seem so . . . resigned," he said. "Aren't you afraid at all?"

She considered it, as the dreamy languor began to take her. No, she already knew how it would be. She only wanted it to be soon.

4

As the undertow carried Embri out, she gave no more thought to those on the shore. She allowed herself to be buffeted by the current until the constriction inside her became a torment that threatened to burst, then surfaced to breathe in shallow gasps. She should give herself wholly to the water, she knew, but a last vestige of doubt blocked her. What if, after all, reality was a suffocating death?

The shadow of a skyhunter swept dark across the sky. It circled back to her and dove, great black wings rushing.

Terrified, unthinking, she spiraled down to safety. Without volition her gills opened and she felt new life flow through her, nourishing her blood and calming the wild beating of her heart.

Her body was free from every twinge and stiffness and pressure. Her eyes, that had been so sensitive to light, saw clearly in the underwater dusk: silver-crusted rocky formations that extended from the shore, swirls of luminous seagrass and a forest of larger, waving fronds that shimmered in a myriad of shades from black to purple to palest green.

She had never known such ease of movement. Sleek and supple, she glided between jagged spires and peered into the fissured mouths of caves. Bolder, she headed out into the open ocean where she raced for hours, celebrating her new strength and testing its limits.

When she began to tire, she descended to depths where heaviness wrapped about her like a blanket. She drifted in darkness, everything within her slowed, in a state that was like sleep.

Later—how much, she didn't know—she became aware of something wrong: a disturbance in the water that told her she was no longer alone.

The other presence was approaching fast. Without seeing it, she knew it was huge—thrice her size—and that it signaled danger.

She fled, angling steeply back up to the light. She lost her pursuer in the dimly lit midregions, but she continued to rise, to what seemed now to be her zone of refuge.

She surfaced into biting air and the glare of two suns. Far above, her other enemy still circled.

She sank with relief into her own world. Here was safety —providing she was vigilant—and comfort. And a duty that began to fill her with a nagging insistence.

She turned back to the shore, to the rocks and feeding grounds where old memories told her she would find her charges.

They were there, and they knew her. At once they surrounded her: swift flashes of motion; seeking, curious.

Too young yet to receive a song. But hers to comfort, reassure, guard. Later, they would listen.

A dark shape swam out from behind a rock. This one was no menace, however—it was only jealous. It circled the feeding hatchlings, cutting them off to its own care.

Embri sent respectful greetings. Nithrin acknowledged them, and after an interval of continued wariness, moved to allow Embri equal access to the hatchlings.

Embri relaxed. There would be no strain between them now. They were both guardians, and both were needed.

Two teachers, with two different songs. Embri guessed what Nithrin would be singing when the time came. Her songs would be of feasts and warmth and indolent days. She would recapture the pleasures of mating and fine houses and shining ornaments, of privacy and one's own space.

They were true songs, and Embri had no quarrel with them. But hers would be just as true. They welled up in her, thrumming to be released.

The earth is brown in the long field,
A stooped figure drags a heavy stick,
Another places seeds in the furrow;
Both are covered with sweat, though the sun gives little
    warmth.

Over the mountains it is summer,
Harvest in the golden grain valley,
Aching backs and sore hands,
But much laughter.

In the Sonsi village a clothmaker pounds her bark,
Dipped from a trough of green bubbles;
Her house is full of friends;
Fishheads rot in a pile outside the door.

The sun comes up over the forest,
Alone without its partner,
Glinting from snow-covered branches,
Before gray clouds obscure it.

Over the white ground,
A stalker: silent, muffled,
Creeps up to the snowgreb mound;
A flurry of digging and scattering,
A sudden grab and a capture.

Firelight on a loved face,
The smell of roasting grain cakes,
While outside the storm roars,
And a youngling sleeps in a corner.